Into

Into The Night

A Novel

By

Darryl A. Perkins

Into The Night

<u>Acknowledgements</u>

This book is dedicated to the men and women who work in our national parks and forests, and to the biologists and researchers whose quest for knowledge greatly enriches all of our lives.

First, I'd like to thank my daughter Suzanne Smith and her friend Ashelin Currie. Both took time out from busy schedules while pursuing their PhD's, to do the initial reading and editing for this book. Thanks also to my sister, Artie "Puddin" Logan, who has always shown unwavering support and confidence in me. In addition, special thanks to Mr. Jon D'Arpino. Jon, who is currently the editor of the Journal of the North American Falconers' Association, provided the final edit for this project and I am greatly indebted to him for his professionalism and advice. Furthermore, special thanks to my two biggest fans: Marva Lynne Flowers and Dr. Titus Plomaritis for their encouragement.

And last but not least, a special thanks to Caroline!

Introduction

Intent on feeding, they paid no attention to the foreign sound of the approaching helicopter. Located in the McKenzie Valley in Canada's Northwest Territories, the pack had just pulled down a bull caribou. Now nine wolves strong, this pack was led by a large black male and his grey colored mate.

Following the lead of the alpha male, the pack bolted for the timber when the helicopter came over the trees and descended upon them like a great bird of prey.

The alpha female felt a sting in her shoulder caused by the tranquilizer dart and moments later, slumped slowly into the soft snow.

Two hours later, after being deemed healthy and pregnant by Dr. Caroline Glenn and her team of researchers; alpha wolf #1 was boarded on a cargo plane and headed to a new life in Montana...

Chapter 1
The Pissant Gos

S he had this way of licking her lips and smiling that has mesmerized me since the first day we met during our freshmen year at Winston Salem State University in North Carolina in 1972.

So here we were thirty years and two children later at a goshawk nest in Great Barrington Massachusetts. Caroline was all smiles as I warned her to be alert. This female was notorious for her aggressive defense of the nest. But where was she?

As soon as we were within 100 feet of the nest tree the tiercel (male) started kaking and doing flybys. That was his M.O. Make a lot of noise and do an occasional shallow flyby but nothing serious. On the other hand, the hen was downright dangerous. Normally you couldn't get within a half mile of the nest before this little piss ant of a goshawk was trying to knock your head off. To be such a little bird, this female was famous for her attacks and had sent many an unwary hiker to the emergency room, but now she was absent.

Not that she advertised her presence mind you. Besides being little and nasty, she was silent. The tiercel would distract you with flybys and kaking, and the next thing you knew you were being blindsided by 30 ounces of enraged fury. In my opinion, getting cold cocked was a small price to pay for the chance at flying one of the Pissant's babies.

To a bird, they were all extremely large, heavy-footed aggressive goshawks that were more than a match for any denizen of the boreal forest, arid desert, or fruited plain. But for whatever reason, old P.A. was missing. Or so we thought.

Chapter 2
Brown Sugar

"Hurry up before she shows up," I said to Caroline.

She handed me her ever-present lollipop, licked her lips and said, "Patience Boo. If she comes she comes."

She licked her lips again as she bent over to adjust the climbing spikes and I couldn't help but smile.

"If you don't quit licking those lips and smiling, you might not ever make it up the tree," I said as I gave her a playful slap on the rump.

"And if you don't quit playing, you might have a decision to make right here and now, my Boo," Caroline replied.

She then faced me with her hands on her hips and smiled.

"What's it gonna be, a pissant baby goshawk or me?" Caroline said.

"You know me baby," I replied. "I choose brown sugar over a goshawk any day of the week."

I walked over and put my arms around her and kissed her lightly on those luscious lips. I then pulled her close and whispered in her ear, "But it's up the tree today darling."

She pushed me away and pretended to pout. I laughed and winked at her and as always, she licked her lips and winked back.

Watching her lick her lips and smile as she got ready to climb the tree caused me to reminisce about the day we first met.

Chapter 3
WSSU

I T was 1972 – the beginning of my freshman year at Winston Salem State University in North Carolina. I was sitting in the cafeteria with my new roommates – Zack Graham from High Point; James "Teeter" Gray from Trenton; and Vince "Pimp" Snodgrass from Jacksonville when in walked a group of four freshmen girls. We had seen them together during orientation so we knew they were freshmen too.

"Ugh! All fine," my friend Teeter said.
"Dang!" Pimp added. "I can't decide which one I want."

We all fell out laughing at that declaration. Vincent Eugene Snodgrass Jr. was a skinny, bifocal-wearing, pimply-faced nerd who also was a self proclaimed-lover, or as he phrased it, a "pimp." His favorite saying was,

"The only reason I ain't hooked up with one of these honeys right now is I can't decide which one I want."

"The boy ain't got no sense," I said. "But give him credit, he's got confidence."

And truth be known, everyone referred to him as "Pimp" not because of his prowess with the ladies, or not even because he had the word "Pimp" enclosed in double quotes and stenciled on the back of the blue jean jacket he always wore. We called him Pimp because someone had referred to him as a "walking pimple" our first day on campus.

"Well, I'll take that little light-skinned one," Zack said. "You know I love red bones."
"They don't want us," Teeter said. "We ain't got no money. We ain't got no car. We ain't got no crib to take them to even if we could pull them right now. We're freshmen. What those girls are looking for is upper classmen with money, cars, and a crib!"

Pimp got up from the table, adjusted the collar on his jean jacket, took the toothpick out of his mouth and placed it behind his ear, and without ever taking his eyes off the girls said, "Relax young'uns, and watch the pimp of all pimps work."

We all started to laugh because we had witnessed this scenario before. Time after time, he would saunter over to a group of ladies and go into his speech. Pretty soon you'd see one, if not all of the girls shaking their heads no. Then the "pimp of all pimps" would return with some lame excuse talking 'bout how they wanted to get with him, but either they just weren't his type, or he couldn't make up his mind which one he wanted.

He walked up to the girls, who had gotten their trays by this time and were just getting ready to eat, and started talking, or as he liked to say, "running his game." He turned, looked at us and then turned back to the girls and said something else. Whatever he said made them all giggle. To our surprise he sat down at their table and continued to talk.

Eventually he returned to our table with a devious look on his face and sat down.

"Did you children learn anything?" he said with that silly smirk still on his face.

I said, "So what's your excuse this time pimp of all pimps?"

"I got no excuse home boy," Pimp said.

"Matter of fact, see that girl with the straight black hair? Her name is Charlene and the Pimpster's gonna be between them legs at seven o'clock, this night!"

"Oh yeah?" I said. "And I guess you're also gonna wake up rich and six feet tall in the morning."

"You got no faith DG. That's why you ain't got a woman. Zack," he continued. "The little light-skinned girl is Reba and she said you could come see her at the dorm tonight."

He turned to Teeter and said, "The tall girl went to Wilson High Teeter. She said she saw you when Wilson played Trenton in basketball. I told her you wanted to meet her and she said to buzz her down to the lobby tonight. She's in Atkins, and as to you my friend," he said, turning to me, "Looks like you SOL. I tried to hook you up with that fine mama with the big fro, but unfortunately for you, she's dating the quarterback of the football team. I told her you were the king of Bushtown, but she still said no thanks. So let's see. Star quarterback or the King of Bushtown? S-O-R-R-Y!"

"I don't need you to give me no hookup. If I want to I'll hook myself up. The ratio's seven to one my man, I'll do alright," I said. "But let me get this straight. Charlene, who, as far as I can tell, ain't blind, is going to let a retard she just met get between her legs? Ain't no way!"

"OK," Pimp said. "Check this. If before they leave, I prove I'm gonna be between them legs tonight, will you give me five dollars?"

"You do that and I'll give you TEN dollars right now!" I replied.

A few minutes later the girls finished eating and stopped by our table before heading out the door. Pimp stood up and introduced us all and the girl that wanted nothing to do with me had the whitest teeth and prettiest lips I have ever seen. She said her name was Caroline and licked her lips and smiled when we were introduced. Right then and there I was smitten for the duration.

Charlene stuck out her palm to Pimp and said, "Where's the money? You said you'd pay me five dollars now to braid your hair tonight."

He smiled, turned to me and stuck out his hand. I gave him my best - you've lost your ever-loving mind look and said, "No way!"

He said, "You don't braid hair standing up homeboy. How we going to do this Charlene? I'm going to lie on your bed while you braid my hair?"

"You wish," she said. "You're going to come over and sit on the steps outside the dorm and I'm going to sit on the steps and braid your hair."

"You gonna sit on the same step as me?" he asked with a grin.

Charlene looked at us and said, "Is there something wrong with your friend? You're gonna sit on one step; I'm going to sit on the next step up. You're going to lean back between my legs and I'm going to braid your hair. If, and only if, you got the five dollars."

Zack and Teeter were doubled over laughing as I handed Pimp my last ten dollars. He handed one five dollar bill to Charlene and shoved the other one in his pocket.

He put that blasted toothpick back in his mouth and winked at me.

"Live and learn young'un. Live and learn," he said before following the girls out the door.

I sat there dumbfounded as Zack and Teeter continued to laugh. The only reason I didn't go after Pimp and take my five dollars back was because I couldn't get the image of Caroline out of my mind.

That was the Friday before Labor Day and classes were to start the following Tuesday.

My first class was Bio 103, Intro To Zoology, in the science building. This was to be my first step toward becoming the greatest zoologist the world has ever known and I couldn't wait to get started.

Class started at 8:15 and I walked through the doors promptly at 7:45. This was heaven. There were the requisite lab tables, Bunsen burners, and frogs in a jar one would expect to find in a zoology class, but this one was special. What set this one apart was the plethora of stuffed animals that adorned the room. There was a bobcat, a badger, a huge timber wolf, and a number of stuffed birds in the room. And to top it all off, there standing next to the wolf and in front of a stuffed red-tailed hawk was my future wife. I whispered to myself, "Thank You Lord."

She was stroking the breast of the hawk as if it were still alive. I strolled over trying to look all upperclass-manish while desperately searching for something witty to say. Fate smiled on me and she spoke first.

"I love wolves and I love hawks, especially red-tailed hawks," she said. "They're both so majestic and so wild. I get a thrill out of seeing the hawks soar. I'm from Missouri and once I saw one catch a squirrel in our back yard."

"A wolf?" I asked while pretending to

"Squirrels?" I said. "I thought they ate worms or beetles."

She looked at me and flashed that beautiful smile and chuckled.

"So you think raptors eat worms. And you are taking this class becauseee...?" she said.

"I'm taking this class because I want to be a zoologist and work with animals at a zoo or do field research or something," I said. "I didn't realize that knowing the dietary habits of red-tailed hawks was a pre-requisite. Tell me something. Does your boyfriend like red-tails?"

"What's that got to do with anything?" Caroline said.

"Well, if your boyfriend doesn't like red-tails, then you've obviously got the wrong boyfriend."

This caused the smile to disappear and she seemed a little annoyed.

"At least he knows what they eat," she said. "And I'm guessing you think that a wannabe zoologist would make a better boyfriend."

"Actually, I was thinking more like husband, but you gotta start somewhere," I replied.

Without another word she turned away and headed for her desk. I quickly ran after her and caught her ever so gently by the elbow.

"Wait," I said. "I'm just teasing you, I'm not proposing. Man, are all the girls from Missouri so sensitive? Before you answer let me ask you a serious question. Do you really love Redtails?"

"I love all animals but especially wolves and especially Redtails. I can sit for hours watching them at the zoo," she said.

"I'll tell you what," I said. "If you're game, on Saturday morning I'll show you something truly amazing. You don't want to miss something that could change your life forever."

"Wow," she said. "I would sure hate to miss an amazing life-changing experience, but there is a football game Saturday you know. We're playing Shaw."

"The game's not until three o'clock," I said. "If you want, I'll have you back in plenty of time to see your Boo play."

"OK, but it's not a date," she said.

"Does that mean that I don't have to pay for lunch or just that I don't get a kiss afterwards?" I asked.

She shrugged her shoulders and said, "It means both. You don't have to pay for lunch and there definitely will be no kiss."

"Let's shake," I said, and offered her my hand. We shook hands and I knew that, after Saturday, she would be mine forever.

Chapter 4
Spike

I had been driving on the back roads of Caldwell County for almost an hour. I started out on Zack's Fork road and traveled south to Kings Creek. Having no luck there, I cut across Dug Hill then turned right onto the Tom Dula Road. Heading north on 268, I passed Laytown on my way to Happy Valley.

I had just crossed over 321 onto the Roby Martin Road and was working my way towards Setzer's Creek, when I noticed a lump on a crossbar on one of the utility poles. I stopped the truck and got out the binoculars. There with his back to me was an immature red-tailed hawk - just what I was looking for.

I drove to within fifty yards of him and he didn't budge. In the bed of the truck was a one foot square wire cage with a couple of store bought mice in it. Covering the body of the cage were fifty or so slip nooses tied from 20 lb test monofilament.

Slowly, I got out of the truck and placed the cage alongside the road. I got back in the truck, turned around so I could see where I was going, and started backing up. I had gone about fifty yards when I stopped to see what was happening.

I checked the pole and he was gone. I checked the trap and it was still there. I was disappointed, but the day was young and if I didn't find him again, another one would show up sooner or later. One thing was certain; there were no shortage of red-tailed hawks in western North Carolina.

I was driving back to pick up the trap when, all of a sudden, the trap started moving as if it were trying to escape. That little rascal was lying on his side on the opposite side of the trap with both feet firmly caught in the nooses.

His mouth was open and his wings flared, but he didn't move as I reached down and got him by the legs. At home that evening, he weighed thirty two ounces. Forty-five days later he caught his first squirrel. This was the beginning of my junior year in high school and Spike was my third red-tailed hawk and first male.

Chapter 5
J.P.

Julius Price was the star quarterback for the football team and according to all the pundits and talking heads, was destined for greatness in the NFL.

He was 6'3" and weighed 195 pounds. He ran a 4.2 forty and had a rocket arm. Only his temper and frequent brushes with the law in high school prevented him from signing with big programs like Notre Dame, Alabama, Texas and every other school in the Big-10, Big-12, SEC and ACC. So here he was - a big fish in a small pond at WSSU. By the end of his junior year, he held every passing, rushing, and punt-retuning record in the CIAA and was second only to Steve McNair for touchdowns all time.

Like the rest of us freshmen, Caroline enrolled in the fall semester. However, she came to Winston -Salem in June to stay with her aunt and got a job in the WSSU bookstore. And she being the finest thing on campus, it was only natural that J.P. would hook up with her when the football team reported early for spring practice.

He wasn't very attentive though and never seemed to have time for her. Caroline said he was preparing for the NFL, but I knew for a fact that he was the biggest dorm-hopper on campus. Dorm-hopper was the term used to describe guys who had a girl in every dorm. She did tell me though that he asked about me once.

"What did you say?" I asked.

"I told him you were a classmate and good friend."

"That's a lie," I said. "I'm not falling into the good friend best friend trap. I'm trying to woo you girl."

And I was dead serious. No way was I going to fall into the best friend trap – been there, done that.

"I'll be your best friend after we get married," I said and she just laughed.

The best friend trap was when the girl you wanted told you all her problems and secrets and depended on you for sound advice. That's sound advice about some other guy! You're doomed when your romantic advances are spurned with these words: "I value your friendship too much." Rule number one in the Man's Book is never, ever become a "best friend." Only one in a hundred progress to the next level after being a best friend.

After class on Wednesday night I walked Caroline to her dorm. She stopped at the top of the steps and flashed that brilliant smile and waved goodbye.

"You're starting to like me, aren't you?" I said.

"Bye Darryl," was her only reply.

I turned to walk away and got sucker-punched right in the nose. I dropped like a polled ox and blood was spewing everywhere. Before I could get up, someone was on top me penning my shoulders to the ground. I lost count of the blows I received, but remember hearing Caroline yelling, "Stop J P!"

She even came to help but he brushed her aside and she fell. It's funny how emergencies and stressful situations cause one to reflect on sage advice from the past. My grandpa always said, "Boy, someone got you down and laying a good whooping on you don't turtle. You get one of his fingers in your mouth – way back where those old hard biting teeth are, and you bite the shit out of him. You clamp down hard and I'll guarantee he'll get up off of you. Now you mark my words if he don't."

Before turning to Caroline, he looked down at me and said, "Stay the fuck away from my girl." Next he looked at Caroline and said, "Didn't I tell you to stay away from this hillbilly?"

With my grandpa's words ringing in my ear, I made my move. I grabbed his right wrists with both hands, raised my head up off the ground, and did just like grandpa said; I bit the shit out of the index finger on his throwing hand. I didn't just snap and let go, I pit-bulled that sucker.

J.P screamed, "He's biting my fucking finger off!"

This caused his entourage to come to his rescue and start kicking me like crazy. Through clenched teeth I managed to say, "Tell them to stop or I'll bite it off."

He yelled to his boys, "Stop! Stop or he'll bite my finger off."
Still holding his finger in my teeth, I said, "Now get up off of me."

By this time a crowd had gathered and everyone just looked on in shock. Here was a freshman with a broken nose and blood all down the front of his jacket with the start quarterback's finger in his teeth.

By now JP was really scared. "Don't bite it off...please?" he pleaded.

Still applying a little pressure I said, "Apologize to Caroline."

Caroline was still sitting on the ground where she had fallen. Like everyone else she was in bit of a shock.

"Caroline, I'm sorry," he said. "You can have this fucking hillbilly if you want him."

I really bit down hard and he dropped to his knees. He was trying hard but he couldn't hold back the tears.
  "OK! OK!" he said. "I'm sorry."

I eased up and let him go. He grabbed his injured finger and beat a hasty retreat with his entourage following close behind.

I walked over to Caroline and helped her up.
  "You OK?" I asked.
  "I'm alright," she said. "But you aren't."
  "My head is bloody, but unbowed," I replied.
  "What?" she said.
  "You know," I said. "From the poem Invictus."
  "In the fell clutch of circumstance, I have not winced nor cried aloud. Under the bludgeoning of chance, My head is bloody, but unbowed."
  "So yes, I've seen better days," I said. "But I'm still looking forward to the weekend. Just gotta make sure I have you back in time to see your Boo play."

"I don't see how you can still joke around like this. This isn't funny at all to me," she scolded.

"I'm sorry," I said. "Who would want to see a star football player headed for riches in the NFL, when they could spend time with a broken-nosed nerd who just got his butt kicked in front of the whole campus?"
I winked at her and she just shook her head and smiled.

Two nights later, Pimp and I were walking back to the dorm from the Ram's Den when we got jumped by six big dudes. Although we tried hard, they beat the crap out of us. One of them said, "Don't let that fucker get his hands on you. He'll bite the shit out of you if he gets your finger in his mouth."

This happened two more times during my freshman year. I could never prove it, but I knew J.P. was behind it all.

To the freshman class and a lot of the girls, I was the cult hero who had risked life and limb for his woman's honor. Never mind that Caroline wasn't my woman. On the other hand, I was despised by the football coach, football team and entire athletic department. For, with one bite,

I had single-handedly foiled the Ram's chances of winning the CIAA championship. While J.P. was still a world class athlete and was high on everyone's draft board as a defensive back and punt returner; with a mangled index finger, his pinpoint accuracy was a thing of the past. On two separate occasions I tried to apologize but each time I'd take a butt whipping within two days of the attempt. Finally I just gave up.

The papers said that because of his inaccuracy and inability to play the position at the next level, not being a quarterback would cost him millions in contract earnings and endorsements. To my mind he lost much, much more. He lost Caroline.

Chapter 6
Hibriten

After that first day in class Caroline and I spoke often. Well, she talked often and I mostly listened. She talked of growing up in the Ozarks, about her family and was quick to point out that, while she was an only child, she was in no way spoiled. I tended to agree.

She spoke of becoming a vet, or doing wildlife research, but clearly birds of prey were the thing that really floated her boat. And I must say, that for one who had never handled raptors before, she was quiet knowledgeable.

Talking to her was fun, but those five days leading up to Saturday were the most excruciating I've ever had. Every day I would call my brother John.

"What's his weight?" I'd ask.

"Thirty-one point five," John said.

"I want him dead on at twenty nine," I yelled.

"Relax knucklehead," he said. "Today's Tuesday. He'll be ready on Saturday."

"He better be," I said and hung up.

The one thing I could do was make her laugh. All I had to do would be to start singing or dancing or talking about my family and she'd almost bust a gut. But no matter what, her conversation always seemed to come back to hawks and wolves.

Hibriten High School is nestled at the foot of Hibriten Mountain in Lenoir, North Carolina. On a clear fall day when the thermals are rising, you can see scores of hang gliders circling the mountain like vultures. The plan was to have John take Spike to the top of the mountain and release him on my command.

Finally Saturday came. For two hours Caroline and I drove the winding road of 421 from Winston-Salem to Wilkesboro, and then took 18 on into Lenoir. We passed the time away by counting red-tailed hawks sitting on the power poles along the way. When we finally got to the high school, I saw my grandfathers pickup truck parked in the lower parking lot next to the practice football field.

There were no cell phones back in those days so I depended on my egg-headed brother to be at the right place at the right time.

"Well, what's so amazing about an old truck and a football field?" she asked.

"You'll see," I said. "Be patient."

I reached into the back of the truck and got my glove and a small packet of cut up beef heart. I walked over to Caroline and said, "Here, put this on."

She put the glove on and gave me a puzzled look. I walked up behind her and placed my right hand on her shoulder and said, "I want you to trust me and do exactly as I say. Think you can do that?"

"You're making me nervous," she said.

"Don't be," I said.

Into The Night

I placed a piece of beef heart in her gloved fist and lifted her arm. I leaned in close and whispered, "Keep your eye on the mountain and don't move."

With that I whistled and life as I knew it changed forever.

I saw him as soon as he left my brothers fist. He lifted off and never flapped a wing as a sudden gust lifted him upwards.

"Look," she said. "There's a hawk."
"Shhhh!" I said. "You'll spoil the moment."

I whistled again and Spike folded up and dropped like a stone. I heard her gasp and then she moved a step forward.

"Be still," I said.
"Oh my God," she whispered. "Oh my God!"

Spike leveled out at ground level, then pitched up and stalled right in front of her raised fist and landed lightly on the glove and gobbled down his prize.

I slipped more beef heart into her glove and Spike continued to feed.

"Spike, meet your new mama," I said. "Caroline, meet Spike. Spike is a tiercel or male red-tailed hawk, *Buteo jamaicensis*. He was trapped at 32 ounces and today weighed 29.5 ounces before eating. This is his third season and I plan on releasing him back to the wild in March."

She never spoke a word and when he finished eating I picked him up bare handed and placed him back in his giant hood, which is just a box with a perch in it for traveling.

I was already naming our children when I walked back to her with this Cheshire cat grin on my face. I expected something along the lines of "You are wonderful and yes I want to have your babies followed by a big hug." What I got instead was a big surprise.

She looked furious. She punched me in the shoulder hard - really hard.

"You're a falconer?" she shouted. "I can't believe this. You let me go on and on about raptors and red-tailed hawks like an idiot and you are a falconer? What about that worm and beetle crap?" she continued. "And what am I supposed to do now, just fall into your arms because you're this great falconer?"

Boy was she mad. Her nostrils were flared and she was fuming. She hit me again. Then she stepped forward and pushed me. I stepped backwards and laughed.

"You think it's funny?" she asked, as she pushed me again. I caught her by both wrists and held her firmly. Now her fury seemed to fade and she looked sad. At that moment all I wanted to do was hold her and protect her forever. She lowered her head and said, "I can't believe you're a falconer." I pulled her close to me and lifted her head. I stared into her eyes and said, "Caroline, I'm your falconer." She licked her lips and smiled and I kissed her. No passionate tongue swapping like in the movies. I kissed the top of her head. I kissed her forehead. I kissed her on both cheeks and then I kissed her ever so lightly on the most beautiful lips in the world. And although it was slight, she returned my kiss. There was no lust in this embrace. The way she felt in my arms confirmed what I already knew. This would be the only woman that I would ever love. This was one of those magical moments you read about. Unfortunately, magical moments don't last forever.

"Atta boy! Slipping her the tongue are you?" Which could only mean that my knuckleheaded brother had come down off the mountain?

He walked right up to Caroline and gave her a big bear hug. He then held her at arm's length and said, "She ain't so ugly." He had almost made it to the truck when the glove I threw caught him in the back of the head.

He fired the old truck up and hollered out the window," Hurry up. Grandma made sweet potato pie, but we can't cut it till her precious college baby comes home."

"That idiot was my younger brother John," I said.
"Are you twins?" she asked.

"Heavens no," I said. "I'm eleven months older than him and I have a brain. People do say we look a lot alike though."

Chapter 7
The Test

We got in the car and headed to Grandma's. Grandma and grandpa lived in Bushtown - a rural community where almost everyone was related, and everybody knew everybody else's business.

To get to Bushtown, you had to travel on a one-lane paved road that wound its way uphill for a mile and a half. There were no street lamps, curfews, or secrets in Bushtown. To the residents, it was Bush Hill. There were only four places one could be in Bushtown. Either round the curve, out the road, or up on the hill. The only other alternative was to be down one of the three hollows (*pronounced hollers*) that spiraled off the main road. There was Archie Ray's holler, Mr. Marshall's holler, or

Joe Hendrix's holler. Ask for someone and your reply was likely to sound like this:

"Hey. You seen Bob?"
"He was down Archie Ray's holler earlier but I think he's up on the hill now."
"No, I was just up on the hill. He's probably out the road."

There was no ball field, swimming pool, or recreation center in Bushtown, but it was the greatest place on earth for a young boy to grow up.

When we turned up Bushtown Road Caroline was all smiles as she watched the houses go by.

"Is that your church?" she asked, pointing to the Bushtown Mennonite Brethren Church on the right.

"Yep," I said. "That's Old Bethel and used to be softball field all rolled into one."

"Your brother seems different," Caroline said.

"He is," I replied. "He's brilliant and has total recall about everything he's ever learned. He gets in trouble sometimes because he says exactly what he thinks."

"He thinks I'm ugly?" she asked.

"Heavens no," I said. "What he was really doing was implying that I had described you as being ugly. Helping me get in trouble with you would make his day. It's like you said, he's different. The brilliant part is true though. He has offers from Harvard, Yale, Duke, Columbia and every other college in the country, plus the Pentagon had him try to break into their computer system. It took him all of 45 minutes to break the most secure and sophisticated system in the world."

"I bet he goes to Duke so he can be close to home," she said.

"Are you crazy?" I said. "He's going to the University of North Carolina at Chapel Hill, or, to Winston Salem State University."

"What's wrong with Duke?" Caroline said.

"What's wrong with Duke? Are you an atheist? Questions like that won't move you up the Mrs. Darryl Glenn ladder," I said.

"Oh. One little kiss and now I'm trying to climb the marry Darryl ladder," she said. "And besides, if he's as brilliant as you say, shouldn't he consider all his options?"

"His options, my love," I explained. "Are to go to school where I go, which is HIS preference, or go to Carolina, which is my grandma's preference."

"And what is your preference?" she asked.

"I told him if you like it, I love it. Where ever you choose is ok with me. But like I said, Grandma is a Tar Heel so it's probably going to be Carolina, which is just fine with me. But speaking of Grandma, I gotta warn you. She may take a little getting used to. My mother died from complications related to child birth shortly after John was born. My father was never the same after she died and passed away himself nine months later. The doctor said it was natural causes but grandma said it was from a broken heart. My grandma and grandpa raised us and she's always been super protective of me and super duper protective of John. Nobody, and I mean nobody, will ever be good enough for either one of us," I said. "She pretends to be tough, but inside she's the most loving, giving person I know. So don't be surprised or put off if she's a little standoffish at first."

"Don't worry," Caroline said with a smile. "Since I'm not trolling for husbands, there shouldn't be a problem."

The aroma from grandma's cooking caused my mouth to water as soon as we entered the house. Grandma had her best smile on and greeted Caroline warmly. She smiled when she gave me a hug, but as soon as Caroline wasn't looking; she gave me "the look".

Grandpa remained sitting at the table and after shaking Caroline's hand, turned and gave me the thumbs up sign.

Grandma said, "Come on and sit down. You know your grandfather don't like to wait supper."

This was the standard call to arms in the Perkins household. It was never wait on supper, or wait to eat supper. It was always "your grandfather doesn't like to wait supper."

Just as we were getting ready to sit down John bounded in the back door.

"I put Spike back in his mew because "stupid" here is so in love, he'd let the poor thing bake in the giant hood."

For someone with a photographic memory and total recall, brother John sure was slow when it came to grandma's number one rule. Under no circumstances, and especially not in front of strangers, were we to speak ill about or to each other, not even in jest.

Without waiting for the obligatory reprimand, John said, "I'm sorry Darryl."

"No problem bro," I said. "I love you."

"Love you more," he replied.

"You got any money?" I asked John.

"I got thirty dollars," he said as he reached into his pockets. "Whatcha doing? Taking the princess here to the movies?"

"Might," I said as I took the thirty bucks from him.

Grandma smiled and took grandpa's plate and fixed it just the way he liked. He liked his peas on top of his mashed potatoes. Some folks like their mash potatoes whipped and creamy and some people like them with lumps. Grandpa Perkins liked his with lumps, so lumpy mashed potatoes were standard fare on grandma's table.

Just as I expected, as soon as we started eating, the inquisition began.

"So," she started. "You're Darryl's current girlfriend?"

"She's either his girlfriend or a floozy," my loving brother said. "He was slipping her the tongue at the high school and this is their first date."

I was mortified, but Caroline seemed to take it all in stride. She looked at me said, "Well, Darryl certainly wants me to be his girlfriend, but I haven't quiet decided yet."

"He's just like his daddy," grandma said in a none to pleasant voice. "He never has and never will want for female companionship."

Caroline continued to smile and replied, "So, I'm not the first girlfriend he let his hawk fly to?"

"Lord honey no," grandma said. "You're not the first and I'm sure you're won't be the last."

During this whole exchange, Grandpa never looked up from his plate. But after grandma's last remark he simply looked at her and said, "Mildred." And just like that the inquisition was over.

All through dinner Caroline kept smiling and licking those luscious lips as she ate. Licking her lips was as natural as breathing for Caroline, but seeing her tongue flick out like a live snake, was driving me wild!

The meal proceeded without incident and after two helpings of sweet potato pie; we got ready to get on the road.

John, Caroline, and I were standing on the porch when John put his arm around my shoulder and said, "It's true. The big dummy here has flown his birds to impress girls a hundred times, but he's never let anyone but me hold him or feed him. That is until today." He then walked over to Caroline and said, "I don't know what that means but there you have it."

"Thanks John," she said.

I just looked at John and shook my head. "Help me Lord. My brother's a retard," I said as I got him in a headlock.

47

Caroline glanced at me with this real annoyed look on her face. "You shouldn't use that word retard," she scolded. "I don't like it and besides, he just loaned you thirty dollars."

"OK, I won't ever use it again," I promised. "He didn't loan me thirty dollars though. He gave me thirty dollars."

"What do you mean?" she said.

"We don't loan each other money in our family. If I have it and he wants or needs it, I give it to him. If I don't have it to give, I tell him and he does the same with me. Money will never come between our love. In fact, nothing will."

"John is not just brilliant," I continued. "He's also gifted physically. He holds the state record in the high jump and the 100 yard dash and he's the most sought-after football and basketball player in the state. Dean Smith told grandma that during his official visit to Carolina, all John talked about was his brother. John told Dean Smith that his brother and grandma were the biggest Tar Heel fans on earth and if he (Dean Smith) could convince his brother (me) to transfer to Carolina, he'd sign in a heartbeat."

Caroline gave my grandfather a big hug then turned to my grandmother and said, "Mrs. Perkins, my mother and all my aunts are excellent cooks, but this was about the best meal I've ever eaten.   And for the record, I will be the last."

"Beg your pardon?" Grandma said.

"I WILL be the last girlfriend Darryl ever has."

With that declaration Caroline took my hand and we headed for the car.

"Darryl. Come here!" Grandma demanded. I walked over and as she gave me a hug she whispered in my ear,

"Now don't play the fool with this one.   She's a keeper."

"I won't," I said.

I got in the car, fired her up, and started off the hill. We drove the first few miles in silence until Caroline looked at me and said. "What did she say?"

"Said you passed the test Boo," I replied.

Chapter 8
The Pissant Gos (continued)

S o here we were thirty years and two kids later preparing to take a young goshawk from the nest. At forty-eight Caroline was just as beautiful as the day we met and still the love of my life.

A bad fall years earlier ended my climbing days, but Caroline could still scamper up a tree in spikes with the best of'em.

Her only protection was protective goggles, a leather jacket pulled over a hooded sweatshirt, thick climbing gloves, and a baseball cap. No helmet or other gear for her. Better that she sustain a few bruises and scratches than the parent birds injure their feet while protecting the nest.

"Be careful," I said as she strapped in and started the climb.

"I know," she replied. "Keep your face to the tree."

And, as if on cue, the Pissant made an appearance. I caught a flash of gray out of the corner of my eye as she zoomed past.

"Be careful," I said. "Here she comes."

True to her reputation, the pissant came in full bore and hit Caroline in the back of the head. The higher she climbed the more intense the attacks became.

As Caroline got closer to the nest rim, I shouted, "Put the eagle gauntlet on."

"Gotcha!" she responded and proceeded to change one climbing glove for the thick eagle gauntlet.

With the pissant, whatever came over the edge of the nest was getting bound to and that's all there was to that. When in position Caroline shouted down, "Here goes!"

With that, she eased her left hand up over the rim of the nest. In a flash the pissant flew in and slammed into the glove. While she was busy killing the glove, Caroline managed to grab her by both legs with the other hand.

This may seem a little over the top but with this goshawk, this was the only way. I found this nest five years ago after getting a tip from a horse rider who had been unceremoniously unhorsed by the Pissant. I went to the nest alone just to band the young. When I pulled myself up over the rim of the nest, she bound to my face. In an attempt to dislodge her, I managed to badly twist my knee. The result was facial puncture wounds and lacerations, a torn ACL, and no banded goshawks.

After getting the pissant under control, Caroline managed to herd the three young goshawks into the picnic basked she had tied to her waist. The basket had a rope tied to the handle. The other end of the rope had been thrown over a branch and reached all the way down to the forest floor. Once the young were in the basket, Caroline said, "They're ready."

I lowered the basket with the three young goshawks to the ground. There were two females and one male. I chose the female with the heaviest feet and placed her in another basket. Then I pulled the rope to raise the basket back up to Caroline.

Caroline tipped the basked over once it was back in the nest and the two remaining youngsters scrambled out. She let the basket go, which I lowered to the ground, and then placed two fresh quail in the nest. She then gave the pissant a toss and she promptly flew a few trees over. She did manage to pop Caroline a few times for good measure as she descended the tree, but then flew to the nest and started feeding the young.

"What we going to call her?" Caroline asked when she got down.

"How does PA2 sound?" I replied.

"Sounds good," she said. "Let's get her home. "

"Right," I said. "Just let me tin the tree. We don't want raccoons following your sent to the nest."

Raccoons were notorious nest robbers and would follow a human's scent to the nest at night. By placing a thin piece of sheet metal or tin around the base of the tree, you would prevent the wily critters from being able to get to the nest.

After completing the tinning task, we headed home.

Chapter 9
Home

Home was a four bedroom log cabin set on ten acres in the Berkshires in western Massachusetts - Great Barrington to be exact. We spent a week camping in the Berkshires during the summer of our freshman year and fell in love with the area. We got married between our junior and senior year and bought this place ten years later.

That first year in college was as close as one can get to heaven on earth. Caroline and I just seemed to fit together. For me, it had been love at first sight. It took a few days and a trip to Bushtown for her to see the light, but the die had been cast. We were soul mates and although we wanted nothing more than to spend every minute of every day with each other; we both recognized the independent nature of one another and didn't allow our love to suffocate our own individuality.

At the end of our freshman year, the National Park Service (NPS) was recruiting seasonal employees at historically black colleges and universities (HBCU). The program was designed to expose minorities to possible careers within the park service. Since the idea of a summer spent working outdoors in a national park appealed to both of us, we took the test. As fate would have it, we both scored high on the test and were accepted into the program. I was hired as a Naturalist Interpreter GS-4 grade seasonal employee and assigned to the Peaks of Otter Visitor Center on the Blue Ridge Parkway near Lynchburg, Virginia. And much to my chagrin and her delight, Caroline was hired and told to report to our nation's first national park – Yellowstone.

I spent every summer during my undergraduate years giving guided walks, manning the campground entrance booths, conducting nightly programs on local flora and fauna, and doing research on nesting Cooper's hawks within the park and surrounding Jefferson National Forest while at the Peaks of Otter.

Caroline, on the other hand, found religion when she witnessed a lone wolf pull down an elk calf that first year in Yellowstone's Lamar valley. This was 1972 and (*Canis lupus*), the gray wolf, had been eradicated from Yellowstone for over 50 years. Her report of the predation was met with resistance and skepticism by the other biologist. By the time researchers found the remains of the kill, it had been so scavenged that it was impossible to tell what predator had made the kill. To this day she still maintains that what she saw was not a large coyote, but the one apex predator whose absence alone had an adverse affect on the ecology of greater Yellowstone, the gray wolf.

Caroline's love of raptors never diminished, but it paled in comparison to her love of wolves. Her love proved to be historical as she was one of the lead biologist and driving forces in re-introducing the gray wolf back to its former range in 1995. Dr. Caroline Antoinette Glenn, PhD., is one of the foremost experts on wolf ecology in the world. By most accounts, livestock ranchers near Yellowstone notwithstanding; the wolf re-introduction to greater Yellowstone and Idaho has been a huge success. And in her mind, Yellowstone was also the site of Caroline's one great failure.

Chapter 10
Yellowstone

Spectacular, incredible, breathtaking, wonderful, magnificent, and stunning are words used to describe our nation's, and the world's first national park – Yellowstone.

Whether it's the awesome power of Old Faithful, the breathtaking beauty of Yellowstone Falls, the quiet colors surrounding Morning Glory Pool, or the Serengeti-like lushness of the Lamar Valley; Yellowstone is a kaleidoscope of brilliant colors and wildlife activity unlike any other place on earth.

It was established by the U.S. Congress and signed into law by President Ulysses S. Grant on March 1, 1872. With high mountains, plentiful water, lush valleys and adequate cover, Yellowstone teems with wildlife.

The thing that jumps out at you about Yellowstone is its wildness that can best be seen in its inhabitants – the cougars, coyotes, elk, deer, moose, bison, and both black and grizzly bears. Yet, nothing says wilderness like the howl of a wolf - the one apex predator missing for over 70 years!

Chapter 11
A Legend Returns

Thanks in part to stereotyping in print (*Little Red Riding Hood*) and in film (*Wolf Man, The Howling*); the gray wolf has largely been viewed as a dangerous, bloodthirsty predator. Due to loss of habitat and deliberate extermination programs, including the predator control program carried out by the National Park Service (NPS), by 1926, the gray wolf was totally eliminated from Yellowstone. In 1973, the gray and red wolf was given protection under the Endangered Species Act.

After receiving her Ph.D., from the University Of Minnesota in 1982, Caroline was hired as a research biologist by Yellowstone National Park (YNP). Two years later, she was appointed head of the newly formed Wolf Recovery Team (WRT).

At the same time Caroline was completing her doctorate in wolf ecology, I was completing my doctorate in raptor biology at the University of Minnesota, under the guidance of Dr. Pat Redig of the world renowned Raptor Center.

So it was that Dr. Glenn, Caroline, A. was employed by YNP and assigned to the Wolf Project, and so was Dr. Glenn, Darryl, A. At the time, I was a raptor biologist with the US Fish and Wildlife Service, which has primary responsibility of ensuring compliance with the Endangered Species Act. Politics being what they were, it didn't hurt that I had spent four years doing field research on wolves with Caroline in Minnesota and in Yellowstone. Having the research team of Glenn and Glenn on the project didn't raise any eyebrows. In fact, it was looked upon as a plus.

After years of intense public planning and input, 14 adult wolves were captured in Alberta, Canada, given a thorough examination and shots, fitted with radio tracking collars and released into the greater Yellowstone area (GYA). In 1996 an additional 17 wolves were trapped in British Columbia and also released into the GYA.

Chapter 12
Lamar

The unmistakable sound of a wolf howling roused me from my blissful sleep. Unclad in a double sleeping bag, I felt the heat from Caroline's half naked body pressed against mine.

I nibbled playfully at her ear, which caused a barely audible moan to escape her lips. I traced the contour of her cheek down to her neck with my tongue which caused the moans to increase in volume. I slid my hand under her t-shirt and cupped a breast. I kissed her neck and marveled at how her sleeping nipple immediately sprang to life at my touch. She put both arms around my neck and whispered in that husky voice, "Don't start something you can't finish."

"Stifle yourself woman," I said as I continued to kiss her neck and play with her nipples. "I love the girls. At first they're soft like marsh-mellows, but now they're hard as acorns. Amazing!"

"Let me play with the boys and see how quickly they get hard," she said.

"Stop that," I said, pushing her hands away.

"Quit acting," she said. "Monique said you men liked to have your nipples played with. Let me see."

She laughed and suddenly pushed me over on my back and rolled on top of me. She pulled the t-shirt up over her head and said, "I see my Captain's ready."

"What about foreplay, taking it slow and all that," I protested with a smile.

"You did that last night as I recall, or have you forgotten?" Caroline said.

"I haven't forgotten a thing," I said. "I'm just trying to make my woman happy."

"You want to make your woman happy then shut up," she said. "I can't stand a mouthy man."

I started to say something smart but Caroline eased into position and as usual she had complete control of my body. Soon the Captain and I were taken on a rollercoaster ride of pleasure and all my troubles were swept away. Somewhere in the distance a wolf howled and moments later, I did too.

Afterwards we lay spent on top of the sleeping bag in each other's arms. Caroline slept blissfully while I drifted in and out of consciousness. Some women were overly talkative after making love, while others wanted or needed confirmation that the sex was good. My woman, on the other hand, always fell into a deep sleep even before I did. I am without a doubt, the luckiest "s o b" on the face of the earth. Thank you Lord!

Finally she woke up. To me this was the best part. In the afterglow of our love making and subsequent snooze, sometimes we played this game.

She would prop herself up on one elbow with her cheek in her had, lick her lips and say, "Thank you Mr. Perkins."

"Mr. Perkins is my grandpa thank you very much. I'm Mr. Glenn," I would say.

"I know but you look just like him," she said. "Hold me and tell me about the first time we met."

I would take her in my arms and start telling her a story about the first time I saw her. She would be focused on every word I said and sometimes I'd catch her holding her breath. She would listen intently just as if the stories were true. They all had the same theme, but the story was always different. Sometimes I was a wounded World War II soldier and she was a volunteer nurse. Other times I was a Zulu warrior and would capture her from a neighboring village. There was quite a bit of acting out in the Glenn household and oftentimes foreplay took on the form of role playing.

"OK," I said. "Who are we this time?"
"I'll be a crack ho and you are a heroin addict," she said, and her eyes sparkled like a little kid at Christmas.
"Crack ho and heroin addict it is," I replied.
Then, in as serious a voice as I could muster, I started the tale.

"You were a crack ho who had been in detox for almost three months. There was turnover every two weeks and a new crop of patients would be admitted as another batch exited the facility. Today there were five new patients coming, all men. You and your girls would station yourselves at one of the card tables in the lounge so you could get a good look at the "new meat." You didn't think too much of the little game, but being different didn't work out so well in lock up so you went along anyway."

"How's it look?" one of the girls asked.
"You shit out of luck this time home girl," April, the self-proclaimed leader of the group said. "Hell, they bringing one in here in a straight jacket."

"Heroin was my demon. I hadn't been high in two weeks and getting off the "horse" was killing me. To control my hallucinations and violent outbursts, I had to be restrained in a straitjacket. When I shuffled through the door, bound in the straitjacket, unshaven and with my afro matted with dirt; you took one look at me, snapped your finger then pointed at me and said, "That's him right there. That's the one I want. Now let me catch one of you bitches looking at him and see what happens."

"But I don't cuss," Caroline said, as serious as she could be.

"But you're a crack ho in detox, remember?" I said.

"Oh yeah, I forgot. Keep going, keep going."

"Anyway," I continued, "two weeks later when I had lounge privileges, you walked up to the table I was sitting at and introduced yourself."

"I'm Caroline," you said. "Who are you?"

"Darryl Glenn," I replied.

"Well, Darryl Glenn, why do you look so sad?" you asked.

"I don't want to do drugs any more but I will," I said. "As soon as I get out I'll be right back on that junk."

"No you won't," you said.

"Why not?" I asked.

You looked me straight in the eye and said, "Because, I won't let you."

"You promise?" I said.

"I give you my word," you said.

"I'd rather have your heart," I said, and I was dead serious.

"You smiled and licked your lips. Next you placed both hands on the table and leaned over until your face was inches from mine. I noticed a single tear roll down your cheek and your voice quivered when you spoke."

"Take my word now Mr. Glenn," you whispered. "I gave you my heart the minute you shuffled through that door."

"Well my heart just melted. What about my addiction? I said. My own voice starting to break as a single tear slid down my cheek."

"I'll be your addiction," you said. "And you'll be mine."

"You smiled and licked your lips then turned and walked away."

"What did you do?" Caroline asked.

"I wiped the tears from my eyes and repeated what I've said every day of my life since we met thirty years ago. Thank you Lord."

Sometimes at the end of one of my stories her eyes would be a little misty, but this time her cheeks were wet. Without saying anything else, I kissed the tears away.

"That was so precious," she said. "You love me like a woman wants to be loved and then tell me a sweet story like that? Umm! You are the most precious man on earth and I LOVE the ground you walk on."

"If that's the case, how about giving the Captain another going over before this Viagra wears off?" I laughed.

Stealing a line from *Circle of Friends*, she said in her finest Irish voice, "I'll hold it, but I'll not jiggle it about." With that we laughed and headed to the creek to bathe.

After a quick dip in Slough Creek, I started my protest as I was drying Caroline's back.

"By the way," I said. "You do cuss."

"I do not."

"You do," I said. "Last night, as I recall, you told me to..."

"OK. OK." Caroline interrupted as she stuck her fingers in her ears and started screaming, "Not included, not included. Gosh, you are a mouthy man."

"I'm mouthy and you're a curser and your daughter is too."

"That's a lie straight from the pits," she said. "Don't you bad mouth my baby girl. Which one are you talking about anyways?"

"Why, Zenyetta of course. Remember at her wedding? I was standing up there beside her at what was one of, if not THE, most important event of her life. Her best friend and maid of honor Ashelin was crying to beat the band; and what do you suppose your baby girl said?" I asked.

"Oh my God you're right" Caroline said as she doubled over with laughter. "You can see it plain as day if you read her lips on the video – twee, stupid bastard!"

"That girl doesn't have a serious bone in her body," I said.

"And she gets that foolishness from you. Who else but you would quote a line from Dances with Wolves at their wedding?"

"How about her sister Rachael," I said. "At her wedding, while we were sharing a tender father daughter moment alone, I kissed her on the forehead and said I'm going to miss you baby girl."

She looked right into my eyes and didn't crack a smile. "Well," she said. "You always got ya whores."

I cracked up and said, "Woodrow F. Call talking to Augustus near the pecan grove along the creek in Lonesome Dove."
"She kissed me and said - now that's my daddy."

We both laughed because it was true. Both our daughters – Zenyetta Antoinette and Rachael Alexandra Marie were always talking fool talk and making jokes.

"Anyway, "I said. "I'm going to file a complaint. I won't be violated against my will by a mouthy woman with two cussing daughters."
"Hush your bellyaching. The government said you were my husband and I could have my way any time I wanted," she said. "And besides, the way you were howling and carrying on this morning, you'll have every pack within a hundred miles rendezvousing right here, and we won't even have to go look for them."

We dressed and got something to eat before starting the day's work which consisted of tracking the collared wolves of the Druid Peak pack.

"You check the signals and I'll saddle the horses," I said.

"Let's check on my baby first," Caroline said.

"Some baby," I replied. "Your baby tops the scale at 195 pounds. That's huge even by McKenzie Valley standards."

We of course were speaking of Lamar. Lamar was an orphaned McKenzie Valley wolf, *Canis lupus occidentalis* that Caroline had reared from a pup. To add some genetic diversity to the released packs in Yellowstone, his mother was taken from the McKenzie Valley in Canada's Northwest Territories in March while she was heavy with pups. Like the other wolves in the project, she was kept in a 2 acre enclosure at the foot of Druid Peak.

She denned while still in the enclosure and gave birth to four pups. Three females and one whopping big male were whelped on April 27th. Caroline took one look at the male and said, "He' going to be the King of the Lamar Valley."

Yellowstone is prone to violent seasonal storms and sudden changes in weather conditions. One such storm sprang up in early May causing a tree to be uprooted which fell against the holding pen.

This accident caused just enough give in the chain link fence to allow a grizzly to get into the enclosure. The mother and the female pups were all killed. Lamar took refuge in a small crevice in the rock formation and the great bear was unable to reach him.

Caroline, God love her, was convinced that she could raise the pup in such a way that he would not become imprinted or bonded to humans, and then release him as a lone wolf into the GYA. All of the biologists, including myself, were adamant that releasing a human-reared wolf was tantamount to a death sentence.

Joining an established pack was risky business for lone wolves, no matter how they were raised. There was no gray area. Acceptance meant a greater chance for survival, while rejection meant instant death. Wolves are very territorial and do not tolerate trespassers. Caroline knew the risks, but was hopeful that with luck, Lamar would find a dispersing female and they would form a new pack.

"An animal as magnificent as Lamar deserves the chance to pass along his genes. There's no guarantee that he won't be killed by a rival pack, gutted by a bison or kicked in the head by a bull elk," Caroline argued. "But it won't be because he was reared by humans. It will be because he's a wolf, and all wolves lead a rough and dangerous life. Remember 202?" she asked.

Wolf #202 was the alpha male of the Slough Creek Pack. He was one of the most photographed wolves in Yellowstone and the undisputed ruler of the Sloughs. Old #202 strayed into rival Rose Creek pack territory and was caught by the Rosie's and torn to pieces. What's amazing is that this was all caught on film.

So it was that Lamar, all one hundred and ninety five pounds of him, spent the first eight months of his life with Caroline and me in the Berkshires of western Massachusetts.

Lamar was a magnificent animal. His head was nearly two feet wide. He was kept in a one acre enclosure and fed mainly on road killed deer. Occasionally a cull from the local deer breeding farm was released into the enclosure. Lamar had all the makings of an alpha. He was big, strong, and confident and had no problem pulling down a healthy, albeit pen reared deer. Even though great pains were taken to prevent human bonding, somehow, Lamar had a definite connection with Caroline.

He was extremely wary and would move to the far end of the enclosure at the approach of any human. One day I was in the loft and watched from the window as Caroline approached the fence. At first Lamar was nowhere to be seen. Caroline turned and started walking along the outside of the chain link fence. To my astonishment

Lamar came up to the fence and started walking parallel with Caroline. When Caroline stopped, he stopped.

I ran down the steps and out the door. As soon as Lamar saw me he bolted for the far end of the enclosure. Caroline looked at me with that kid caught with her hand in the cookie jar look and dropped her head and walked silently to the cabin.

I stopped at the door and watched her as she got a cup of tea. She sat down at the table and looked at me with sad-puppy eyes.

"How long has this been going on?" I asked, as I joined her at the table.

"Three weeks," she replied.

"What do you mean three weeks? Why didn't you tell me?" I yelled.

"I didn't know what to do. I thought it would stop. He's never shown any fear of me and I've done nothing, absolutely nothing to encourage it," she cried as the tears started to flow.

"Have you been in the enclosure?" I asked and got no reply.

She raised her head and looked at me but said nothing.
"I can't believe you," I said. "You're supposed to be a scientist. One who appreciates and understands nature and yet you let your womanly, feel good emotions guide you and risk all our hard work. All that will do is get him killed one day and it'll be your fault. You should be on Oprah or Dr. Phil, not heading a wolf recovery team in Yellowstone!"

I regretted what I said but it was too late by then.
"You sexist prick," she fumed. "I didn't go into the freaking cage to pet or kiss him. You weren't here. You were supposed to retrieve the carcass remember. You told me that only you would drag the kill into the enclosure and you promised to be home before the state delivered the road kill. So what happens? You're God knows where chasing your precious goshawk and I'm stuck with a freshly killed deer carcass bleeding in the driveway."

"Lamar was out of sight at the far end of the enclosure, or so I thought when I drug the carcass through the gate. That new wolf, #43 that was trapped in Maine, was behind the mound as usual. All of a sudden something hit me from behind and I went down. There was this sharp pain in my shoulder and I realized that #43 had me by the shoulder. I was kicking and screaming when out of nowhere Lamar appears. He got #43 at the base of the skull and honest to God Darryl, I heard the bones as Lamar crushed his spine."

"I thought it was a skirmish over the carcass and Lamar, being an alpha, had killed #43 in a dominance/food dispute. This proves one thing," I said. "As sure as twice one is two, #43 was raised by people. Habituated wolves cannot be trusted. End of story. What happened next?"

"Promise me you will never mention it to a soul," she said.

"I give you my heart," I said.

"Negro, I got your heart. Give me your word," she demanded.

"You have my word," I said.

"It was unbelievable. Forty three is a 95-pound male and there stood Lamar with #43 dangling from his jaws like he was a rag doll. So I'm between Lamar and the kill, and Lamar is between me and the gate. As I watched him, all my fear seemed to fade away. He dropped #43 and howled. I remained frozen until I noticed the blood trickling down from my hand. I had forgotten that #43 had given my shoulder a pretty good shaking. Lamar walked up to me and licked my hand once, then started feeding as if I weren't there. I walked out and locked the enclosure behind me."

"Amazing," I said. "But that doesn't alter the fact that he can never be released."

"Wait," she said. "There's more. Remember when I told you I had a funny feeling someone has been watching me."

"Yeah," I said. "I checked it out the last time and did find a single set of tracks but more than likely it was a hiker or fisherman."

"I know," Caroline said. "But what I didn't tell you is that each time Lamar goes crazy. He paces and lunges at the fence while keeping up a constant growl. Someone is up to no good and Lamar can sense it."

"So now you're telling me Lamar is your private protector and can sense evil before it happens," I said.

"You see," she said. "That's why I didn't tell you. You're a wonderful man, Darryl Glenn and a lot more sensitive than most, but at the end of the day, you're still just a man. Because you can't quantify everything that's happened and report it in the Man's Journal; you dismiss it as female hormonal nonsense. I love you, but sometimes you're a pig-headed, conservative asshole of the highest order."

"Aha!" I said. "I was just waiting for the conservative label to get thrown into the mix. But on a serious note, forgive me for the Oprah-Dr Phil comment. Perhaps a little male jealousy reared its ugly head. I'm sorry. You are my queen and I adore you, but what are we going to do about Lamar?"

"Nothing," she said. "He's wary, if not downright fearful of every human except me. If you're even in the yard he's so fearful of you that he doesn't know that I even exist. Agreed?" she asked.

"Agreed," I said. "But here's the rule. No walks along the gate. That just encourages him and strengthens the bond. I'll take the kills into the pen from now on or it stays outside. Comprende?"

"Si," she replied.

"Makeup sex?" I inquired.

"What do you think?" she said, and turned and walked away.

"Well, that explains one thing," I said.

"What's that?" she asked.

"Now I know why you wanted to be on top so much these past three weeks. I thought you just wanted to, shall we say, ride Sally ride, but you were really protecting your injured shoulder," I said. "Did you at least go to the emergency room?"

"No. I called Titus and he came by and stitched me up."

Titus Eagleritus was our good friend and surgeon from nearby Lenox, Massachusetts.

"I'm going to have some words with that snake in the grass," I said.

"You will not," Caroline said. "I made him promise not to tell you and he made me give him my word that I wouldn't go into the enclosure again."

"Let me get this straight," I said. "You break your word to me about going into the pen, but you honor your word to some surgeon. Is that right?"

Caroline walked up to me, put her arms around my neck and gave me a peck on the lips. She then laughed and said, "Wa, wa, wa. Stop you whining. I knew you were mouthy, but I didn't know you were a whiner."

"I give up," I said, and kissed her on the forehead.

That was two years ago and so far it seems that Caroline was right. We took Lamar from the Berkshires to Yellowstone and kept him in a release pen for a month. Upon his release, Lamar or wolf #302 as he was officially known, managed to avoid being killed by any of the established packs. Later, he paired with Soda Butte female #135 and raised five pups. Last year, they raised seven pups bringing the total for the Druid Peak pack to twelve. The number would have been 14, but one of the first year pups drowned and one of the yearlings was shot.

You would think that, ten years after the project started, it would be smooth sailing now. The meeting in Helena two nights ago proved otherwise.

Chapter 13

Exposed

Ralph R. Wilcox, Jr. lay prone on the ground atop the mesa overlooking the valley. He had his spotting scope focused on the timberline. It was here last week that he had seen that big son-of-a-bitch lead the pack on an elk chase. They were out of range that day, but today he had the scope mounted Browning T-Bolt chambered in .22-250. The shot would be about 200 yards, but thanks to his sniper training while in the service; this would be a piece of cake. He had been here since just before sunup and was reaching for the thermos when he caught movement to the west.

"Well well, what do we have here?" he whispered to himself.

"Looks like the wolf lady from Yellowstone is here trying to track some of her wolves. Damn," he thought. "This is going to mess up my plans."

To his surprise, she got down off the horse, leaned her head back, cupped her hands around her mouth and howled just like one of those freaking wolves. She repeated the action and soon there was a reply coming from the timber. The next thing he saw was the biggest monster of a wolf ever bound out of the timber and run right up to the wolf lady. It reared up on its hind legs and placed its paws on her shoulder. His huge body dwarfed her as she grabbed him by the neck.

Spellbound, Ralph continued to watch as she opened the beast's mouth to examine his teeth. After examining his teeth she checked his collar. In the distance a wolf howled and the monster turned and without ever looking over its shoulder, disappeared back into the timber. The wolf lady mounted up and rode away.

Ralph had seen her out riding before and noticed that she always had the same red plaid mackinaw wool jacket and floppy hat on.

His mind was working overtime as he rode back to the ranch. Now he had proof that these were different wolves. They had all been told that these wolves were afraid of people and were in no way habituated during the reintroduction process. When he reached the ranch he dismounted and walked to the bunk house.

"Where's Pedro?" he demanded.

"Here boss," came the answer from the corner of the room. "Need something?"

"Come with me," Ralph said.

Pedro was a trusted hand and had proved himself loyal on many a capper in the past. Ralph told him what he had seen and what his plans were.

"When?" Pedro asked.

"While we're at the meeting in Helena," Ralph replied.

"I'll stir up a stink."

"Gotcha," Pedro said, and with that he returned to the bunkhouse.

Chapter 14
Helena

Long before the first wolves were released into Yellowstone, public hearings were set up in various towns in Wyoming, Montana, and Idaho. The purpose was to allow for input from the public so the project team could address their concerns, as well as afford the project the opportunity to educate and inform the public of the necessity of wolves in the Yellowstone ecology.

There were two opposite groups at the meetings. There were the folks who thought the wolf could do no wrong, and those who thought wolves were bloodthirsty demons that would kill their children in the night.

Tonight's gathering in Helena was one in a series of scheduled meetings designed to update the public on the status of the project. Among others, at this particular meeting was a prominent rancher, Ralph Wilcox Sr. of the Bar-W ranch. Mr. Wilcox had lost two heifers this past week to wolves. The wolves in question, numbers #106 and #211 were eliminated by the Predator Control branch of the Dept of Agriculture. This action infuriated the wolf lovers and did nothing to placate those against the re-introduction.

As head of the project, Caroline made her opening statement. "Ladies and gentlemen, I want to thank each of you for attending this public meeting. We're here to receive input from you and to give you an update on the status of the re-introduction project. Rather than bore you with statistics, charts and maps; let me just say that by all accounts, this re-introduction has been one of the most successful conservation/restoration efforts in the history of this country. On the back table are copies of the fore mentioned charts and maps. With me tonight are my colleagues Drs. Dave Smith, wolf biologist with Yellowstone National Park, and Darryl Glenn with the US

Fish and Wildlife Service. With that being said, I'll open the floor for comments. I would ask that you limit your comments to four to five minutes and please allow the comments to go uninterrupted."

Ralph Wilcox had no ax to grind with wolves. He was all for re-introduction, but not at the risk of his cattle. He had shot wolves caught in the act of killing his livestock and reported the shootings according to the rules laid out in the Endangered Species Act. His son, Ralph Jr., was a horse of a different color. Junior, or King Ralph, as he was locally known, was a bully who vowed to shoot every wolf on his ranch. He was fond of saying, "Having wolves shoved down our damn throats is one thing, but having them shoved down our throats by an uppity bitch from back east is another." I know it was unprofessional, but my only hope was that he'd make that statement in front of me.

"Our ranch and every other ranch around Yellowstone are being overrun with your damn wolves," Junior began. "We just lost two more heifers that we know of last week and who knows how many others the damn varmints have killed that we didn't find. There ain't a small dog or a big dog for that matter, that's still alive that ain't kept indoors. Hell, they use to have a dog problem over in Bozeman before the wolves were let go, but now you can't find a stray at all. Another thing -- these ain't the same wolves were here in the old days. I saw a big sumbitch the other day and he went 300 pounds at least. These are some steroid-fed experimental wolves that don't get sick and have huge litters. What I want to know is when are you gonna take them off the endangered species list so we can shoot'em on sight?"

That got the crowd all fired up. Caroline stood up, and in a very calm voice said, "Let me address your concerns one at a time Mr. Wilcox. First, there are no 300 pound wolves. The largest wolf on record weighs 195 pounds. If you examine the handouts, you'll find that while there was an increase in the overall populations between 1995 and 2004, due to disease, there was a significant drop the past two years. As has been stated in the past, the wolves used in the reintroduction were trapped in Alberta and British Columbia, Canada and are not steroid-fed or genetically engineered. With respect to livestock loss, we knew this was going to happen. However, provisions have been made to compensate the livestock owner for his loss, plus the offending wolves were eliminated. If and when they are removed from the endangered species list, the states will have to get federal approval on a management plan which will not, I assure you, contain a shoot on site provision. But let me get this clear. Am I to understand that it is your contention that one of the benefits of wolf introduction is elimination of the stray dog problem in Bozeman and is thus a cost benefit to the town?"

"Hell no!" he said. "And don't go twisting my words you uppity bitch!"

I jumped up from the table and had to be restrained by Dave, but his comments didn't sit too well with others in the crowd either and they let him know it.

"I'm sorry," he said and stalked out the door.

The meeting proceeded with all parties being very passionate. Wolves seemed to bring out the passion in people one way or another.

I was still seething by Junior's comments as we gathered up the material.

"These people just don't get it," I said. "The wolf has a right to be here. It's better for the environment. It's better for the park. How can we get these backwoods farmers to realize it?"

Caroline stopped what she was doing and looked at me long and hard. I knew from experience that when she did that, she was just trying to control her temper before speaking. Finally she said, "I should remove you from the project. In fact, unless you can convince me otherwise, consider yourself removed. I'll let your boss know in the morning."

I started to smile but could see she was dead serious.

"What did I do?" I said.

"You're an idiot," she said. "You got some groups like Defenders of All Things Wild, who want a wolf on every corner. You got your Ralph Wilcox, Jr's of the world who think the only good wolf is a dead wolf. You got conscientious ranchers like Ralph, Sr., who understand the importance of wolves; yet must weigh their impact against his livelihood. And then there are the members of the team. The biologists and scientists whose job it is to try and find some middle ground between all these warring factions, and who must realize that it is not political agendas that's important here, but the wolves themselves. It's the wolves stupid. It's the wolves and the contributions they are making to the wellbeing of the Yellowstone ecology. And by the way, noted biologists shouldn't let their pea sized brains get overloaded with testosterone causing their judgment to be flawed just because their woman gets disrespected by some local jerk. It's unprofessional."

"You don't love me," I said and put on my hurt puppy look.

"Here we go," she said.

"You don't," I said. "If you loved me you'd always let me be right. If I mess up you're supposed to grin and bear it and then let me have my way in the back of the pickup to boost my spirits."

"You're unbelievable," she said and then licked her lips and smiled.

We held hands and walked to the truck and then noticed a tall figure standing in the shadows. When he stepped out into the light we saw it was Ralph Jr. I felt Caroline squeeze my hand and she whispered, "Be good. Please."

He waited for us and we stopped in front of him. He looked at me and said, "Look, I owe you an apology. I didn't mean to call your bitch uppity."

He was expecting a charge or swing by me, but what he didn't expect was to get hit flush on the nose by the corner of one of those government-issue binders. Thank God for Julius Price and the sucker punch. When Caroline hit him, Ralph dropped to one knee holding his broken nose with blood pouring all over the ground.

"Why you uppity b..," was all he got to say before she kicked him right between the legs. This caused me to flinch and Ralph toppled over on his side. And I swear to God she was getting ready to kick him in the face when I dragged her away.

"Caroline! Caroline!" I said. "Calm down now. You don't want to kill him."

After a minute, she had her temper under control and we walked over to where Ralph was just pulling himself up off the ground. He spat some blood on the ground and said, "I don't fight women. You let your woman do your fighting for you?"

Caroline answered, "You lucky it was me. He would have bitten the shit out of you." She turned and walked to the truck.

"She hates rude behavior in a man," I said. "She won't tolerate it," and started walking to the truck.

"You two had best watch your back. I won't forget this," he said.

I was halfway to the truck and stopped dead in my tracks when I heard what he said. I turned and started walking back to him when Caroline ran between us and pushed me back towards the truck. She said, "Please baby, let's just go."

"I'm only going to talk to him" I said. "I give you my word."

She let me go and I walked back to Ralph. I said, "I'm only going to say this once cocksucker. You mess with my wife and I'll kill you in the open."

I got in the truck and Caroline slid over beside me like a high school sweet heart. She leaned over and kissed me on the cheek.

"We'll talk about this tomorrow," she said. "I want you on your back as soon as we get to the cabin."

"Yes ma'am," I replied.

"Did I hear you quoting Woodrow F. Call from Lonesome Dove?" she asked.

"You did," I said.

"You won't do," she laughed and leaned her head on my shoulder.

Chapter 15
Tragedy

It was routine for me to saddle the horses while Caroline checked the signals. We had four of the Druid Peak pack collared and were conducting daily tracking to see the range of their established territory.

"Have you seen my jacket and hat?" Caroline asked.

"Nope," I said. "What do I tell you? Make preparations for the next day. You're hardheaded. Your mother told me you wouldn't listen."

"Darryl," she said. "Someone broke into the cabin."

"And took what?" I asked.

"My coat and hat," she replied. "Nothing else is missing that I can tell."

"That's weird," I said. "Why would someone go to all the trouble of coming way up here, break into the cabin, steal a worthless hat and coat and ignore the laptops, GPS systems, and expensive spotting scopes? That doesn't make sense."

"I know," she said. "But that's what happened. You ready?"

"Ready if you are," I replied.

"I saw 42 two days ago near the Lamar river," Caroline said. "Let's check her first." With that Caroline adjusted the receiver to wolf #42's frequency and got a strong beep one second apart. This indicated that she was within a mile so we started riding in the direction of the signal.

We had ridden about half a mile when she checked the signal again. It was still strong and still pointing in the direction of the Lamar River. As we were riding up the mountain to a ridge adjacent to the river, Caroline checked the signal for other wolves in the pack.

"They're all coming from the same direction," she said. "They must be on a kill or at a rendezvous site."

"Is your baby with the clan?" I asked.

"I haven't checked yet," she said. "Gonna check on him right now."

I continued to ride until I noticed that she was no longer following me. I turned in the saddle to see what was keeping her. She was standing up in the stirrups with the Yagi antenna pointed in the direction of the mesa near Soda Butte.

"Darryl?"

"What baby?" I said.

"Have you got your receiver?"

"Sure," I said, and I noted the concern in her voice.

"Can you turn it on Lamar's frequency please?" she requested.

I got the portable Tracker receiver out of the saddle bags and hit the switch. I had all the collar frequencies pre set and punched in channel #1, which was frequency 216.055 – Lamar's collar. Instead of the one beep per second I expected, I got a beep that lasted for four seconds then was silent for two before emitting another four second burst. The transmitter issued this type beep when the animal had been motionless for three hours. It was known as a mortality beep.

Slowly I rode back to Caroline.
"It could be a malfunction. He could have gotten it off. It could be anything," I said.

Caroline didn't even acknowledge that I was there. She just started riding in the direction of the signal. We rode on in silence for three miles then descended to the valley below, crossed Slough Creek and headed for the timber. The signal was booming so we knew that Lamar, or at least his collar, was just beyond the trees. I saw what I thought was Caroline's jacket laying on the ground. Caroline saw it at the same time. She raced past me and slid her horse to a stop just before the jacket.

Her jacket was covering the dead body of Lamar and her hat, with a note pinned to it, was lying nearby. Caroline was sobbing quietly now as she handed me the note. The note read, "He thought I was you until I blew his fucking brains out."

"I killed him," Caroline wept as I took her in my arms. "Just as sure as if I had fired the shot myself. You said it yourself the day Lamar killed 43. You said one day this connection would get him killed and it would be my fault and you were right."

She was sobbing uncontrollably and I knew that no amount of talking could console her now so I held her and let her cry it out. After a while she stopped crying and I kissed away her tears. She looked up at me and said again, "You were right. I got him killed."

"Darling," I began. "Myself and every other biologist on this project were wrong. You took a human-reared wolf and released him alone into Yellowstone. Not only did he survive for four years, but he thrived. He functioned as an alpha in the most successful and aggressive pack in Yellowstone. And, except for when he was radio tracked and darted from the helicopter for re-collaring; Lamar was never, ever photographed. He's the infamous wolf number 302, the most human shy wolf in all of Yellowstone. No disrespect to Dr. Mesch, but what you did is unprecedented. And the proof is not in Lamar himself, but in his genes which are flowing throughout the Greater Yellowstone Area. Dr. Smith told me that his son, #321 from that first litter, tops the scales at 225 pounds. It's true that Lamar is gone, but his legacy is your legacy and it's alive and well in Yellowstone."

"That's why I love you," she said. "You have this way of making everything right."

"I love you too," I said. "You want a moment before we take him back?"

"Yes, and Darryl..."

"What baby?"

"Thanks."

"You bet," I said. "Now wouldn't be a good time to ask for a poke would it?"

She just looked at me and shook her head. "Is there ever a time when fool talk doesn't come out your pie hole?"

"Well," I continued. "It says right there in the Man's book that when you're weak, distraught, hurt or crying – is an ideal time to offer a little loving."

"Is it offering loving or taking advantage?" she said.

"Makes no difference to us men," I said. "Not as long as the final destination is a poke." I got tickled and fell out laughing.

"You know," Caroline said. "When I first told my mother about you I said you were different. You didn't have a big ego. You didn't let the Captain do your thinking for you. You didn't have to constantly prove your manhood. You would love and support me and not be jealous of my accomplishments. I said you were kind and considerate and I was the luckiest girl in the world."

"And what did my loving mother-in-law say?" I asked.

"She said darling I'm sure he's all that, but remember this. He's still just a man and the smartest of them creatures is still dumb as a bucket of nails."

"I don't believe you," I said.

"Okay," Caroline said. "She said baby girl, even if you're heartbroken because you lost a good friend, or, even if you doubt yourself because something didn't go your way; or you're so sick you can't hold your head up -no matter what, always let your man have his way whenever he wants."

"Amen!" I shouted. "Girl you was raised right."

I walked over and kissed her on the forehead. "Take your time," I said and left her to say her goodbye.

Chapter 16

The King is Dead

This was a piece of cake. Pedro jimmied the ancient lock on the back door and let himself in. As instructed he didn't touch anything. He picked up the hat and coat from the peg inside the kitchen door and left without leaving a trace.

He was a slightly built man and the wolf lady's coat fit perfectly. He rode down off the mesa, chambered a round into the Winchester lever action 30-30 and howled. He waited a few minutes and howled again. This time there was a reply so he sat the saddle and waited.

Like all wolves, Lamar saw with his nose. That is, he of course saw what he saw with his eyes, but he verified what he saw with his nose. He recognized the form sitting on the horse but still circled downwind to catch her scent. When the breeze flowing down off Druid Peak brought Caroline's familiar sent to his quivering nostrils, he started trotting boldly towards the one human he trusted.

Pedro saw him when he came out of the timber. "Man, Ralph was right," he thought. This was the biggest frigging wolf he had ever seen and he'd killed a bunch since the re-introduction. He wanted to be certain of the shot, but he didn't want that monster to get too close. Since the wolf was traveling directly into the wind, the horse hadn't caught its scent yet. Best get it done before the wind switches.

When the wolf was fifty yards away Pedro grunted like a buck deer. This caused the wolf to stop dead in his tracks and Pedro sent a hollow point round directly between his eyes.

Just like that the King of the Lamar Valley was dead.

Chapter 17
John

It was no secret that my brother John was different. It was certainly no secret that he was extremely gifted and brilliant. Basically, John did what I did. That's not to say that he wasn't an independent thinker. He was. It's just that we enjoyed doing the same sorts of things and always did them together.

Falconry is and always has been my passion. I live and breathe it. John, on the other hand, is an accomplished falconer because of who he is, not because of what it means to him.

I'll never forget his senior year in high school. Some guy had sent him a prairie falcon that had spent years in a breeding project. We were discussing her over the phone one evening and John had commented how difficult it was to get her to go up. In falconry, getting your falcon to "go up" means to get her to fly high into the sky. A high flying falcon has an advantage over the quarry – usually ducks or grouse – and affords the falconer the opportunity to witness her stoop or dive out of the heavens. Everyday, John would take her to this large field and fly her, but she never got more than treetop high. She would circle a few times and then John would call her to the lure. The lure was a piece of leather at the end of a four or five foot length of rope or string. There were straps sewn into the lure from which you could tie small pieces of meat. When the falconer wanted to retrieve the bird, he would simply swing the lure which the falcon would grab or foot.

"It's simple," I said. "Does she love the lure?"
"Oh, she'll come a mile to the lure," John said.
"Well, just hang the lure off one of the clouds and let her fly up there to get it," I laughed.

He was silent for a few minutes and I thought for certain that he was thinking of some smart comeback. Instead he said, "That might work. I gotta go," and hung up.

Three weeks later, Caroline and I drove to Lenoir to have dinner with the folks and John was all excited about something. By this time Caroline and grandma were as thick as thieves, so Caroline went to help in the kitchen.

After our earlier phone conversation about the prairie, John called his best friend Dorsey – Dor for short. Dor Jerguson was an engineering major at North Carolina A&T, whose dream was to become a NASCAR engineer for Dale Earnhardt Racing. It seems that together, the two of them had come up with some sort of new falconry apparatus.

John said, "Come watch the prairie fly."
 "Sure," I said.

We drove to the big field and John got this contraption from the back of the truck. It looked like a huge salt water fishing reel mounted between two blocks of wood. He then got a kite from the truck, attached it to the end of the line on the reel and in seconds the kite was 50 feet in the sky.

"Hit the latch," John instructed. "This will lock the reel and prevent it from letting out anymore line."

I did as I was told and sure enough the reel stopped spinning and the kite was held fast at its present height.

The kite line passed through a Sampo salt water swivel. Next John got a small replica of the lure which was attached to four feet of line by a clothespin. There was another piece of line attached to the clothespin and this loose end he tied to the swivel. He attached the clothespin to the kite line and told me to hit the switch again and let out more line. I did and in no time the kite was up three hundred feet with the lure dangling from the clothespin attached to the kite line.

"Watch this," John said and removed the hood from the prairie falcon. She cocked her head and looked at the lure, then left John's fist and began climbing to the lure. In no time she was there and grabbed the lure. When she grabbed the lure the clothespin was jerked free of the kite line. She couldn't fly away because the other end of the line that was attached to the clothespin was tied to the swivel. The end result is that the swivel slid down the kite line as the falcon continued to try and fly away. It worked like a charm and I was dumbfounded.

I just looked at my brother and said, "You are amazing. I make a joke about attaching the lure to a cloud and in three weeks you've invented something that will revolutionize falconry forever!"

I was going on and on about how the invention of using a kite to train a falcon was brilliant. How this should be patented. John just smiled and said, "Shhhh. You'll spoil the moment."

Years later some falconer in California would take credit for inventing the kiting method of training falcons, but my brother Jon, and his buddy Dor did it back in 1973.

Yes John was different and nobody loved him or knew him like I did. But even I was shocked when at super he announced where he would be attending college.

I headed back to the house while John fed the falcon.

Grandma, grandpa, Caroline and I were all sitting around the table waiting for John to finish washing up in the bathroom. Grandpa was hungry because he said, "I'll bless the food Mildred."

Nothing gave my grandma more pleasure than to have all of us around the table as she thanked her Lord and Savior Jesus Christ for the blessings He was about to bestow upon us His unworthy children. Most times the blessings went a minimum of five minutes and if grandpa didn't cough, could go on for ten minutes or more. My grandpa didn't play. I don't care if grandma prayed for an hour, we were to sit with our heads bowed and not fidget or check our watches and we better not look impatient at the end of the prayer. We were to all chime in with a hearty a-man at the end of the prayer coupled with looks of thanks and appreciation on our faces. Grandpa didn't say a lot, but what he said he meant. But if he was hungry, as was the case today, he would offer the blessing.

So when John finally came to the table we held hands and grandpa blessed the food.

"Dear Lord make us true and thankful for what we're about to receive for the nourishment of our bodies. Bless the food and bless the hands that made this food possible. Amen!"

After everyone had gotten their plates filled, John made the announcement.

"Well," he started. "I've decided where I'm going to college."

I immediately started chanting, "Tar Heels, Tar Heels, Tar Heels!"

"Nope," he said. "I'm going to attend the Naval Academy."

"Why the Naval Academy?" Caroline asked.

"Because I think it will give me the best opportunity to prepare for what I want to do with my life," Jonathan replied.

"And what might that be?" grandma asked.

"To serve my country," John said and started digging into to grandma's macaroni and cheese, which was his favorite food.

"Well," grandma said, with an obvious look of disappointment on her face.

My grandpa didn't say a word. He merely looked at John and nodded his approval. I could see the pride in his eyes though and unless I was mistaken, a tear was trying to decide whether to stay put or revel itself and take the long cheek slide. Grandpa served in the navy during WWII.

As for me, I knew immediately that the navy and this country as a whole had just gotten considerably better.

John entered the naval academy at Annapolis in the summer, and as I knew he would, he excelled. By the end of his junior year he had successfully completed the navy's elite SEAL (Sea, Air and Land) training. The following summer, he finished number one in the sniper training program. His hope was to be commissioned and assigned to a Seal team upon graduation.

Unfortunately, John had been tracked by the Pentagon since high school and his earlier work with their secure data systems. Because of his high intelligence scores, the fact that he was fluent in Russian, Spanish, Arabic, French, Italian, and German, and was a computer whiz kid to boot; made him quiet attractive to the FBI and CIA. Much to his chagrin, after graduation, instead of being assigned to a SEAL team, he was offered his choice of assignments between counter terrorism with the FBI, or as an intelligence officer with the CIA. He chose the FBI.

So it was that in the summer of 1977, having graduated from the US Naval Academy with honors, my baby brother reported to the FBI Academy located on 385 wooded acres on a Marine Corps base in Quantico, Virginia—about 36 miles outside Washington, D.C.

John focused on special firearms training, counter-intelligence, behavioral science, crime scene investigations, and fingerprint and criminal history record training. His first assignment was as an instructor at the International Law Enforcement Academy, or ILEA—a global training ground for police executives and criminal justice leaders from Eastern Europe and Asia that was run by the FBI and the Hungarian government with the help of many partner nations and agencies. The ILEA is housed in the former barracks of the Royal Hungarian mounted police, deep in the heart of historic Budapest.

Chapter 18
Smoke Jensen

After Lamar's death Caroline and I completed our research and returned to Great Barrington. Caroline was working on her book about wolf recovery and I had accepted a part-time teaching assignment at UMass Amherst.

One day around lunch time my secretary buzzed in.
"There's a Mr. Smoke Jensen here to see you," she said.
"Send him right in," I said and started to laugh.

Smoke Jensen was a character in a paperback western series that John and I both loved. Smoke was lightning-fast with a gun and didn't tolerate rude behavior. Smoke Jensen was also a name that both John and I used when we didn't wish to reveal our true names.

John came through the door with dark shades and a full beard.

"Why Mr. Jensen," I said. "I hardly recognize you."

"With that gut you've got, I hardly recognize you either," he smiled and embraced me in a bear hug.

"I thought you were in Budapest teaching the girls the counterclockwise double swirl technique," I said.

"I came to hire you. According to Caroline, you're the king of the counterclockwise double swirl," he laughed. "I don't have long," he continued and handed me a flip up cell phone.

"So here's the deal. I'm going to be out of pocket for a while. If you need me use this cell phone. Grandma has one too, but she doesn't know what it's for. There's a bug under that lamp in your living room. Don't let Caroline get rid of the lamp. I had your house and buildings swept for bugs and everything is clean. This bug is so I can keep tabs on you. It is also sensitive to the placement of any additional bugs on the property. Someone tries to bug you place, I'll know it in seconds. My official file says that I am an only child so you, Caroline and the kids, and grandma and grandpa are all safe but you can never be too sure. Any questions?"

"No. I know the routine by now. You be safe brother. I love you."

"Love you more," he said, and with that he kissed me on the cheek and walked out the door.

I didn't ask questions because I knew better. Sometimes I'd get a call with instructions to go watch CNN. There I would see some rescue or disaster and would know where John was and what he was up to. Other than that, when he was out of pocket, I would just wait to hear from him again while grandma had the prayer warriors out in full force.

Chapter 19
Into The Night

Returning from Yellowstone, Caroline and I settled into a nice routine. Life was good in western Massachusetts and I was happy and content sharing this time with the love of my life. Our evenings were spent watching movies or taking quiet walks on the property.

Before we left Yellowstone, in the name of scientific research, Caroline was given one of Lamar's cubs to raise. She was to totally habituate the pup to humans and then see if it could make the transition to wild wolf. In reality, this pup was to replace Lamar and had the blessing of the Secretary of The Interior.

Wolf #404 was a 225 pound replica of his father. He wore a tracking collar at all times and had a GPS chip implanted just under the skin on his back. At night, Caroline and Mac – short for McKenzie Valley – would often take long walks in the forest. Even though we lived in a rugged, desolate area; I never feared for Caroline's safety as long as Mac was with her.

Aside from Mac, Caroline carried a can of pepper spray and a Kahr P9 which is a polymer grip version of the Kahr 9 mm pistol. Thanks to John, she was an expert.

To the west of our property, was a farmer who ran about 40 head of sheep. Lately, he was losing livestock to what he first thought were coyotes, but later proved to be feral dogs. One evening after supper, I accompanied Caroline and Mac on their nightly walk. It was a clear night with the moon shinning bright as we followed a path that led to the pond near the western border of our property. Caroline and I were walking side by side and Mac was a few yards in front of us. As we got closer to the point where we could see the lights from our neighbor through the trees, Mac stopped. He raised his head as if testing the breeze and a low growl rumbled from deep within. Then all hell broke loose as the sounds of sheep bleating, cursing from our neighbor and a shotgun blast filled the night. We heard rustling up ahead and knew that someone or something was headed straight for us.

Soon the cause of all the commotion was revealed as three dogs came barreling down the path. They saw us and put on the brakes. There was a large shepherd-mix with blood on his muzzle, a collie and what appeared to be some sort of husky. The collie and husky turned off the trail and raced up the hill. The shepherd actually barred his fangs and took a step in our direction.

Since he was a pup, Mac had been conditioned to ignore sheep, chickens and most domestic animals. The one thing that no amount of conditioning, exposure, or pleading could change was his out and out hatred of dogs. Given the opportunity, Mac would kill every dog he encountered. Before the Sheppard could decide whether to fight or flee, Mac had smothered him and was shaking the life out of him.

Realizing that these were the sheep killers Caroline sprang into action. In a second the P9 was in her hand and she got off two rounds so fast that it almost sounded like one shot. The two escaping dogs were about thirty yards away and going all out when each one dropped in mid stride.

We heard the bushes moving and swearing like you've never heard before and knew that our neighbor, Bud Searcy, was headed our way. He came stumbling down the path with only one shoulder of his trademark bib overhauls fastened. Caroline was relieved to see that Bud had come alone. Usually he had two old hounds with him when he was chasing them damn sheep killers. He stopped to catch his breath and surveyed the scene.

"Hell. You Glenn's have solved all my problems. I owe you a big thank you!"

"Glad to help, Mr. Searcy," Caroline said.

"Hell, call me Bud," he said. "Me and Ruby don't visit often but ever you need us, just give a damn holler. The boys are always asking about you down at the feed store. I told them the other day, I said, now them Glenn's are funny bastards it's true. She traipses around with the biggest gol-dang wolf ever been born, and he flies them ah grey ghosts we call'em and them bastards'll knock your head off if you get near the nest. Anyway, I'm much obliged to you for killing these sheep killers. They've been giving me fits. Now listen, Ruby's got a pot of mutton stew on the stove and she's the best by God cook in the Berkshires if I do say so myself. Come on over and have a bowl."

"Will she have some tomorrow?" Caroline asked.

"Hell, we'll be eating on it all week," he replied.

"Then how about tomorrow night," Caroline said. "I need to get Mac back to the house. He's okay around sheep but he hates all dogs."

Bud looked at Mac and said. "Well, he's a big sumbitch alright, but I'll tell you what, you bring him on over and we'll see what happens. The boys may be getting a little long in the tooth, but they're still feisty. I figure together, Jake and Jim will give him a good ass whooping' and then everybody'll be friends. Sides, we'll all be right there and if they get to giving it to him too hard, we'll just pull'em off. Long as you promise not to plug them like you did these three sheep killing bastards."

"Caroline only shot two dogs Mr. Searcy, I mean Bud," I said. "Mac killed the big one."

"You mean the time it took me to get here from my place he killed that Sheppard?"

"By the time you heard Caroline shoot, the Sheppard was already dead. I think it best that Caroline and I come alone tomorrow night," I said.

"Damn, I guess so," he said. "I'm gonna let the sheriff and paper know the sheep killers are dead. Me and the little woman will be expecting you tomorrow night to supper."

We headed back to the house. I had my arm around Caroline's shoulder and she had her arm around my waist.

"So," I said. "How does it feel to be referred to as a funny bastard and then be invited to supper?"

"Well, I been called worse, and besides, I sort of took it as a compliment."

"And to think that Ralph Wilcox Jr. called you uppity," I laughed.

"Don't mention his name to me. My tolerance only goes so far."

When we got back to the house Caroline said, "You go on in. I'm going to see to Mac first."

"OK," I said, and walked over and gave her a kiss on the forehead.

I knew Caroline was going to be a while with Mac.

"I'm an idiot," I thought to myself. "I never should have mentioned Ralph Wilcox." I'm sure tonight brought back memories of Lamar and wouldn't be surprised if she and Mac took another short walk. I would take a long hot bath and give her some space.

I filled the tub and put my favorite fragrance from Bath and Body Works in the water. I had fixed myself a cup of green tea, which thanks to Caroline, I had learned to enjoy. I had become accustomed to the taste and actually it was good for my colon. I thought to myself as I eased into the steamy water, "God how I love that woman. I can't even begin to imagine life without her. Thank you Lord."

I had dozed off to sleep while enjoying the warmth of the water when I heard Caroline enter the bathroom.

"Ouuu," she said. "I need to shave my legs."

"Make sure that's the only thing you shave," I said. "You know I'm a bush man of the Kalahari and like my women natural. None of that Brazilian wax crap for me."

"Why yessuh Massa," Caroline said. "Me ands yo other wenches be sure we keeps our self nice and bushy just the way you likes Massa. Is I pleasing nuff to you Massa? Cause iffin sompin you don't like I sho gonna change it lickety split!"

"Girl, if I've said it once, I've said it a million times. You been raised right!"

"Does Massa want to be sleeping by himself tonight on the couch?"

"You don't love me," I whimpered.

"Here we go," she said. "If I loved you I'd let you be the master and I'd be your slave wench, right? If I really loved you, I'd obey your every command, correct? Poor baby. I'm so sorry you married an uppity black woman who speaks her mind."

"See," I said. "You don't love me. You back talk and everything. That's what's wrong with the world today. We black men don't get the respect and support we deserve from our black women."

"On no you didn't!" she fired back, snapping her fingers and waiving her hands in the air. "It ain't support you black men want - it's submission. We let you make decisions to keep your manhood up. Then, when it doesn't work out, we're supposed to ignore it so as not to damage you ego. You're all a bunch of mama's boys. It's always someone else's fault for your failures – it's the system, it's the man, it's getting no respect and support from your black women. If we speak our minds or disagree with you we're being disrespectful or we don't love you."

"Hey," I said. "Are we role playing here or arguing?"

"You might be role playing but I'm pissed."

"What did I do?" I asked.

"Look, I know you like a full bush, but I'm sick of this bush man of the Kalahari crap. Just how many women you got anyway? They said on Dr. Phil when a man teases about his women or what he likes or what he isn't getting at home then he's trying to tell you something and you better believe him. You say little things like my women this and my women that as if you're teasing, but I think you're trying to tell me something. And you, like most men, will throw a hissy fit if we so much as compliment another man in a magazine. Oh it's ok for you men to talk about Beyonces' butt or Jay Lo's behind, but let us mention Denzel and y'all get plum jealous. Then, to beat all that; you whine about not getting respect from your black women, when half you cocksuckers aren't with a sister in the first place! So let's just put all the cards on the table. Now I'm asking, how many frigging women with unshaved crotches do you have playa?"

She was standing there next to the tub with her hands on her hips. Her nostrils were flared and she had the look of the pure devil in her eyes. There were little blotches of spittle at the corner of her mouth which meant she was really pissed. I thought there for a minute she was gonna slap me.

"Girl-I-I-I," I said and laughed. "You almost had me but using the "CS" word gave you away."

"You're a girly boy," she said and fell out laughing. "I did have you. You were about to cry. If you were a Mandingo warrior instead of a little girly boy you would have said, shut your pie hole woman and get your ass in this tub."

"Shut your pie hole woman and get that big butt in this tub," I said.

"Now don't go too far," she said. Was that big necessary?"

"Suppose I said get that big beautiful scrumptious butt of yours in this tub now?" I asked.

"That's much, much better she replied," as she slid down between my legs with her back resting against my chest. I wrapped my arms around her and she twisted her head around and gave me a long slow kiss.

"Tell me a story," she said.

"About what?" I asked.

"We're seventh graders," she said.

"OK," I said. "We were in the fifth grade and I had known you all my life. You had five brothers and they were all my friends. I played ball with your brothers and spent the night at your house on many occasions but never really paid any attention to you at all. Once when we were in the third grade, some of my friends and I was playing marbles. You came along and said "picks up" and grabbed my marble and started to run. I remember popping you in the nose when I caught you."

"You hit a little girl?" Caroline asked.

"I was in the third grade," I said. "And you had just grabbed my marbles. Anyway, grandma gave me the spanking of my life right in front of you and I had to apologize and give you my favorite marble. After that, every chance you got you would stick your tongue out at me. I hated girls and I especially hated you. If you had been somewhere playing with a doll like you were supposed to be, then none of this would have ever happened and I'd still have my favorite marble. We didn't have a swimming pool, or recreation center in our little town, but we did play softball in the church parking lot. Mind you, the church parking lot wasn't paved so it was ideal for a softball game. By the time we were in the fifth grade you quit being the enemy and became a competitor. I played shortstop and so did you. Everyone said that you were the best shortstop and that really got under my skin. Most of the time, we played on opposite teams. When we were picked for the same team I was quick to call shortstop. Made no difference though, sure as shooting someone would say let Repiks play shortstop – that was your nickname back then - and you play the outfield, Darryl. You know you got a stronger arm than she does. You would look all smug, but would stick your tongue out at me as soon as no one was looking. Boy, I hated your guts."

"So when did it change?" Caroline asked.

"Shhhh," I said. "You'll ruin the moment."

"I remember we were in the seventh grade. We were all walking up the road one day after Bible School. You and your cousin Sugar Pop were walking up ahead of me and my cousin, Morris. He looked at you and said, "Looks like Miss Caroline is starting to get a little shape on her. Your girlfriend is growing up DG."

"What do you mean girlfriend? " I said. "I don't even like her."

"Who you kidding," he said. "Everybody knows you two love each other. All that competition between you two – you can't stand her and she can't stand you only means one thing – love my friend."

"The next day you were walking past my house and I said,"Hold up. Where you going?"

"To Miss Bessie's store," you said.

"Wait a minute and I'll go with you," I said. "You didn't say anything, but you waited. You had on this little silk like yellow mini skirt and your hair was fixed real nice. I said, I'm a better short stop than you girl."

"My name isn't girl," you said. "And who cares if you're a better shortstop than me."

"Well, I care," I said. After that I didn't know what else to say. I was prepared to argue about who was the best shortstop, but was at a loss for words now. It was very awkward until I blurted out, "You're going to be my girlfriend one day."

"You stopped and looked at me and just shuck your head."

"Boys are so dumb," you said and kept walking.

"Why did you say that?" I asked.

"Cause I've been your girlfriend since fifth grade, dummy."

"Well if you're my girlfriend, then can I hold your hand?"

"Yes, you can hold my hand and you can buy me a bottle of pop when we get to the store."

"OK," I said and we held hands as we walked to the store. And you know what? I got the same butterflies in my stomach then, as I do right now."

"Not so fast big boy. I feel something poking me in my back, but finish the story."

"From that day on we were inseparable. Either I was at your house or you were at mine and it remained that way all through high school. We even made a pact that we wouldn't have sex until after we were married."

"And did we remain true to our pact and live happily ever after?"

"No. I messed up. I discovered sex and got another girl pregnant. You never got over it and ended up marrying someone else."

"Awwwww! That's sad," Caroline said. "I thought we would be together forever."

"Well, if it makes you feel any better," I said. "I never stopped loving you."

Caroline turned around in the tub and said, "Is that right? Now who is this woman that you've loved all your life?"

"Are you crazy?" I said. "You asked me to make up a story and I did."

"Negro please, you don't make up a story like that. I could see your reflection in the mirror and you were remembering someone. You even looked a little sad at one point. Even the Captain's gotten melancholy. One minute he's poking me in my back and the next he's a sad puppy. Look at him," she said. "Say what you want mister, but I WILL be giving your grandma a call, Bud!"

That night our love making was sweet and tender. Afterwards I lay awake all night as she slept nestled in my arms. When she opened her eyes I was staring at her face.

"Did you sleep at all last night," she asked.

"No," I said. "I just wanted to hold you and listen to you breathe. What's my favorite song?"

"Ecstasy by the Ohio Players," she answered.

"Why?" I said.

"Because that's what was playing on the radio in my dorm the first time we made love. That was at the beginning of our sophomore year in 1973," she said.

"I told all my boys that I hit it our freshman year five days after we met," I said and laughed.

"You told the truth," Caroline said. "It was five - exactly 365 days from the time we met," she chuckled.

"And what did I say that night?" I asked.

"You said that loving me was ecstasy to you and that you would never, ever leave me," she said.

"You mean I said that after being with you only one time?"

"Ah, that's what good loving will do to you my brother," she boasted.

"Those may be the words from the Ohio Players, but they said exactly what I felt then and still feel. Loving you, Caroline Antoinette Glenn, has been pure ecstasy to me, and I thank God for your love every day of my life."

"Promise me something?" she asked.

"Anything," I replied.

"You won't ever leave me."

"Darling, I give you my word, I will never, ever leave you," I promised.

"And what is MY favorite song?" she asked.

"That's easy. The Rose, by Bette Midler," I replied.

"And why is that, might I ask?" she said.

"Because according to you, it is the most beautiful words to any song ever written, and it describes exactly how you feel about me," I answered.

"Sing it for me?" she said.

"You know I will," I said.

"Some say love, it is a river, that drowns, the tender reed."

"Some say love, it is a razor, that leads the soul to bleed."

"Some say love, it is a hunger, an endless burning need."

"I say love, it is a flower, and you, it's only seed."

"Play that at my funeral," she said.

"I won't be at your funeral," I replied.

"Now Darryl, don't you start that foolishness," she said. "If I go before you – you WILL be at my small memorial service, and you WILL play The Rose!"

"Be kinda hard from inside your casket," I said and I wasn't smiling. I know it's foolish but I just couldn't bring myself to talk about arrangements or last wishes with her. I just couldn't bear the thought of life without her. When she started these conversations, I would say,

"When you go, I go. You in a casket, I'm in a casket." I had gotten up and walked over by the window.

"No casket. I want to be cremated, remember?"

"Why are we talking about this?" I said. "I sing the Rose to you and the next thing I know you're talking about being cremated. Is my singing that bad?"

"I'm sorry Boo," she said, holding out her arms to me. "Come here and let mama hold you."

I walked over and laid back down on the bed. She put one arm across my chest, threw one leg across my thighs, and then kissed me on my neck.

"Look," she said. "I think the boys are getting hard."

"You play too much," I said and got up and stalked into the kitchen.

"Come back here my Zulu warrior! I want a poke!" she shouted. "I promise I won't mess with the boys." Then she started laughing so hard tears were in her eyes.

"You play too much," I said and went into the bathroom to shower locking the door behind me. I could hear her laughing from within the shower.

We had a quiet breakfast and spent the morning listening to the Ohio Players, Bootsy's Rubber Band, and AWB. We reminisced about our college days, the birth of our girls, and talked about how blessed we were to have each other. She got up to put the dishes away and I said what I always say, "Thank you Lord!"

That night, promptly at seven o'clock, we knocked on the Searcy's door. The two old hounds were lying on the porch when we pulled up. One, I don't know which, raised his head up and bawled one time. The other one managed to thump his tail against the wooden floor a time or two, but that was the extent of their greeting.

Caroline had already given me my instructions before we left the house, but reminded me again once we reached the Searcy's.

"No matter what it looks like, no matter how it smells or tastes; we are going to have this meal with our neighbors and not insult their hospitality. You got it?"

"Yes massuh," I replied and knocked on the door.

Bud Searcy opened the door and said, "Welcome neighbors. I hope the boys didn't give you a hard time when you stepped on the porch."

"They thought about it," I said. "But Caroline has a way with vicious animals so we made it ok."

Bud had on a fresh pair of bibs and a clean tee shirt and I could tell he had combed his beard. I could tell because there were no twigs or particles of past meals sticking out.

Ruby came over and first gave Caroline a big hug and then me. She smelled of fresh lilac and had on a delightful print dress. Actually, the dress matched her dishes. The meal was simple. She heaped our bowls full of mutton stew and had freshly baked bread and a jar of honey on the table.

"How about a little blood of the grape to go along with the meal?" Bud said.

"Sure," we answered in unison.

Ruby got a milk jug from the fridge which contained a dark liquid.

"Don't mind the trappings," Bud said and looked at me. "It's the contents that count. You take a jug of this home with you tonight and it'll put lead in your pencil for sure."

"Searcy!" Miss Ruby scolded. "Mind your manners."

Well I have to tell you. That was the best meal and wine I have ever tasted and I was raised by Mildred Perkins. Before we left I told Miss Ruby, "I come from a long line of good cooks and Miss Ruby, you are at the top of the heap. Feel free to invite me to supper any time."

You could tell she was pleased by the color that was steady growing up her cheeks and the sparkle in her eyes.

"Wait," she said. "I made this for you," and she handed Caroline a pan of gingerbread.

Bud walked over and put his arm around Ruby and said, "We don't get out much. We stay right here on this farm, but I'd live in the middle of frigging New York City or the Piney Woods of Georgia if Ruby wanted to. I'm blessed with the best cooking and loving a man could ever want. Ain't that right Miss Ruby?" he said and he gave her a playful pat on her rump.

"Forgive my swamp Yankee," she said with a big grin. "A little of the juice and mutton stew always makes him feisty. You know how they get," she said and winked at Caroline.

"Lord honey, I do," Caroline laughed. We thanked them and headed out the door.

When we arrived back home I said, "That mutton and wine has me a little feisty too."

Caroline got out of the car and we headed to the steps.
"Wait," Caroline said.

There was something alarming in her voice and I stopped in my tracks.
"What's wrong?" I said.
"Something's not right," she said. "Where's Mac?"
"The gates locked," I said. "He could be at the far end of the enclosure."

"Never have we come home and he's not at the gate," she said. "Something's definitely wrong."

She placed the pan of gingerbread on the hood of the car and started walking towards the pen. I was right on her heels and bent down momentarily to tie my shoes. I remember seeing something wet and gray fall on my hands and drip between my fingers. It's funny how at that moment I wondered why brain matter was falling on my shoes. I looked up and saw Caroline falling back towards me. The back of her head was missing. Seconds later I heard the report from the rifle. The bullet got there long before the sound did. I remember standing up so I could catch her. I did not want her to hit the ground. Something hit my right shoulder with sledge hammer force and I went down. The last thing I remembered before blacking out was the second report from the rifle. It sounded like it was a mile away."

Chapter 20
Sergei

"D amnit!" He was furious with himself. It was supposed to be one shot two kills. Just as he was pulling the trigger, the man bent over and he fired. It was a head shot and clean kill but if the man had remained standing, it would have been a twofer.

He sat motionless for over two hours last night waiting for the woman to come outside. When the man appeared with her, he couldn't believe his good fortune. He had hoped to get two birds with one stone last night, but the sheep killing dogs and blundering neighbor had ruined all that.

If they had proceeded as usual, the man would have headed up the steps first. With the woman following close behind, a head shot for her would have resulted in a spine shot for him. A good piece of work to be sure but nothing compared to the ultimate – one round two head shots he had anticipated.

Carefully he broke down the Cheytac M-200 Intervention rifle. The Cheytac was the ultimate in sniper rifles with a maximum effective range of 2,250 yards. It fires a .408 caliber specially manufactured 305 grain round and comes equipped with an Advanced Ballistic Computer (ABC) that calculates and provides windage and elevation for the operator. The scope for the Cheytac is the Nightforce NXS 5.5 – 22X variable with a 56mm Objective which makes night shooting a walk in the park.

In less than a minute, Sergei had the Cheytac broken down and packed in its carrying case and strapped to his back. To a casual onlooker he would appear as a camper or backpacker. With night vision goggles on, he back tracked three miles through the woods to the car parked in the old cemetery. He had watched the movements of the three town cops for a month and no one ever came near the cemetery.

He headed west on the Mass Pike crossing into New York. He then headed north to private plane hangar in Albany. He had picked out a twin engine Piper Cub and knew that the owner was vacationing in Florida. He got in the plane and after his initial flight check, proceeded to fly to an abandoned private air strip about 5 miles west of LaGuardia.

At LaGuardia he boarded a Swissair flight to Zurich and then took the rail north to the border town of Basel. Basel sits in the northwest portion of Switzerland on the borders of both France and Germany. From a tactical standpoint, Basel was an ideal spot for Sergei to launch his many forays. Not only was Basel the rail hub of Switzerland, but it shared an airport with the French city of Mulhouse and the German city of Freiburg.

Sergei's rented chalet set on a hillside on the west bank of the Rhine River. To the unsuspecting it looked just like any other cottage but it was a virtual fortress. Equipped with motion detectors, modern listening devices, heat sensitive monitors and laser activated alarms; it was a testament to his lifestyle and professionalism.

Before entering the door he checked a pocket receiver. Any warm-bodied creature with a core temperature above 50 degrees inside the chalet would be indicated on his receiver. This little beauty wasn't even available on the open or black market. While trinkets such as these were toys for the ultra-rich and famous – who were his main clients – for someone in his profession, they were absolutely necessary for survival.

Upon entering the chalet he did a thorough check. Everything was in order so he reset all the alarms and settled down with a glass of wine and his laptop.

A quick check of his accounts showed that 1,110,980 Swiss Franc's or $1,000,000.00 American had been wired to his account. All was well.

Chapter 21

Promise

"Come home John. Caroline and Darryl have been shot. She's dead and Darryl's in a coma. Your grandma is worrying herself to death thinking that someone's after you too," the voice on the other end of the phone said. It was filled with hurt and grief.

"I'm on my way grandpa," Jonathan said. "Don't let anyone else talk to Darryl. Tell him to pretend he's still in a coma if he has to."

"Jonathan," grandpa said. "This won't stand boy."

"Don't worry grandpa, this won't stand."

While Jonathan Glenn, or his substitute, was an instructor at the International Law Enforcement Academy in Budapest; Smoke Jensen was conducting covert operations all over the world. When the call came about Caroline and Darryl, he was in a safe house in Seattle, Washington. For two years he and his partner, agent Rebecca Fleming had been trying to flip a member of a known terrorist cell. Just yesterday the target had come over and under the promise of immunity, had agreed to work with the government. He closed the cell phone and said to his partner, "I'm going off the clock. I'm going to need your help from time to time and it all has to be on the DL."

"Whatever you need," Becky said.

"For starters, pull the tax records for Ralph Wilcox, Jr of Helena, Montana for the past ten years. Then check all off shore deposits or wire transfers over a hundred thousand dollars for the past five years. Call me on the secure line when you have something."

"What's going on or is this on a need to know basis?" Becky asked.

"Someone murdered my sister-n-law and tried to kill my brother. It could be someone with an ax to grind against Caroline, or it could be someone from our world trying to get next to me. Either way I can't take any chances with Darryl. Arrange for an open casket memorial service for Darryl a week from today."

"You got it," she said.

"I want surveillance cameras positioned so I can review everyone's face that pauses and looks at the body.

"Done," Becky replied.

"Thanks Rebecca," John said. "I really appreciate your help on this."

"Don't mention it," she said.

He left without saying another word and never noticed the longing in her eyes. They had been assigned to the same project for three years and he didn't have a clue that she was hopelessly in love with him. So far it hadn't interfered with their working relationship, but it was getting harder and harder for her to keep up the charade.

As he was leaving the building he placed a quick call to Blue Star Jets, a private jet charter company that booked private jets for clients.

In the trunk of his car was a pre-packed bag with credit cards, passports, and twenty-five thousand dollars in cash. There was a condo registered to the name of a Mr.

James "Smoke" Jensen in the Back Bay area of Boston that contained everything he would need.

Another quick phone call to field headquarters and arrangements were made to allow him to drive onto the tarmac at Seattle-Tacoma Airport.

An hour later he was waived through by Sea-Tac security and drove up to the waiting Gulfstream 200. The 200 is a medium size luxury jet capable of flying 3,620 nautical miles at speeds of up to .82 Mach (541 mph), at altitudes of up to 41,000 feet.

"Where to Mr. Jensen?" the pilot asked.
"Logan," John replied.

Five hours later he was walking down the corridors to ICU at Beth Israel hospital in Boston. Walking past the nurses' station he noticed one of Boston's finest leaning over the counter obviously trying to make time with one of the nurses. Hopefully this wasn't the guy assigned to protect his brother.

As he continued down the hallway to room IC 13, he saw a young police officer sitting outside the room. As John approached the room the officer stood up.

"Sorry sir, but no one is allowed into this room except family with two types of identification," the young officer said.

"I'm his brother," John replied.

"May I see some identification please?" the officer said.

"Of course, officer...O'Grady is it?" John asked.

"Yes sir," Officer O'Grady replied.

"Here you go," John said, producing his passport and FBI identification badge.

"Thank you sir," Officer O'Grady said. "Would you happen to have a driver's license?"

"I do," John replied. "Is it standard procedures to request three forms of identification?"

"No sir, but it's at my discretion to request additional information if I feel that the situation warrants it," he said.

"And it's your contention that this situation, namely me, needs to show additional identification? Is that right?"

"Yes sir. My sergeant said better that I inconvenience someone by seeking additional identification, than to let something happen to the person we're guarding," he answered. "So, may I see your driver's license please?"

"Absolutely," John said and handed Officer O'Grady his license.

"Thank you sir," O'Grady said as he opened the door for him.

"Thank you officer," John replied.

Inside, he found his grandpa sitting by his brother's bedside. John walked over and placed his arms around his grandpa's broad shoulders, then leaned over and kissed him on the forehead.

"How is he?" John asked.

"Holding his own," his grandpa replied. "The bullet just missed his lungs, but the doctor said it was such a large round - .50 caliber I believe – that the damage was extensive. They had just been to dinner with the neighbors. They forgot a jug of homemade wine the neighbors had given them and the man, Bud Searcy I believe is the name, found them when he brought the wine over. If it weren't for him Darryl would have bled to death."

"Is he awake yet?" John asked.

"Yes," grandpa said. "He's conscious but he's pretty sedated right now. The doctors don't know it though. He's playing possum till he talks to you."

At that moment I opened my eyes.

"Is that you baby bro?" I asked.

"I'm here," Jonathan replied as he moved to hold my hand.

"I can't kill him," I said. "Whoever did this...," I mumbled trying to stay awake. "I'm way too stove up to kill him right now."

"You won't have to," John said.

"Promise?" Darryl said.

"I promise," John answered.

"How's grandma," John asked.

"Not too good," grandpa said. "I just made her go to the hotel. The girls are with her and they're pitiful."

At the hotel John knocked and Zenyetta opened the door then collapsed in his arms. Alexandra rushed across the room and joined the embrace and she too sobbed uncontrollably.

"We don't have a mama," Zenyetta cried.

"What are we going to do Uncle John?" Alexandra asked through her tears. "Mama's gone."

"You girls listen," John said. "You got a mama. She's just gone now. I ain't going to lie to you. The hurt will lessen, but it will never stop. My mama died when I was less than a month old. I don't remember what she looked like. I don't remember how it feels to have her hold me. I don't remember what her hair felt like or how she smelled, but I ache for her so bad sometimes I can't stand it. They say that time heals all pain, but that ain't true. Like grandma says –time don't heal nothing- but your Lord and Savior Jesus Christ will see you through these hard times. I know you girls got a hole in your heart, but you have your mother's memories; and if you want to see her, you have only to look at each other, or look in a mirror. I know you got your crazy sense of humor from your daddy, but everything else, including your looks; you got from your mother. Except maybe those big honkers you got."

"You leave our noses alone," Zenyetta said as she wiped away the tears.

"You and Daddy look like twins," Alexandra added. "So if we got big honkers like Daddy, then we got big honkers like you."

"Where's grandma?" John asked.
"She's in the other suite," Zenyetta replied.

John knocked on the door leading to the adjoining suite.
"Come in," said a weak, but familiar voice.

John walked in and found her sitting in the recliner reading her bible. Until now, he was a federal agent skilled in the art of espionage and warfare. He was superbly trained and ideally suited for the adrenalin rich lifestyle of high finance and international corruption he had chosen. But today he didn't come here to console his grandmother. Today, he came to be comforted by her as only she could. He was not Jonathan Glenn FBI agent, or his alias Smoke Jensen. He was a ten year old little boy who needed loving assurance from his grandma that everything would be alright.

He knelt down beside the recliner, laid his head on her lap and started crying so hard it was difficult for him to breathe.

"Hush baby," his grandma said as she patted him on the head.

"I will lift up mine eyes unto the hills, from whence cometh my help. My help cometh from the LORD, which made heaven and earth. He will not suffer thy foot to be moved: He that keepeth thee will not slumber," she read.

"Behold, He that keepeth Israel shall neither slumber nor sleep. Do you remember this?" she asked.

"Yes ma'am," he answered as he continued to cry.

"Then help me finish. The LORD is thy keeper: the LORD is thy shade upon thy right hand. "

John replied, "The sun shall not smite thee by day, nor the moon by night."

Grandma continued, "The LORD shall preserve thee from all evil: He shall preserve thy soul."

John answered, "The LORD shall preserve thy going out and thy coming in from this time forth, and even for evermore."

"Now get up and wipe them pretty eyes," grandma said. "You gonna get my apron wet."

John stood up and wiped his eyes. It was just like always. When he was hurt and couldn't stop crying, grandma would quote scripture to him and ask him to help. No matter what, this always worked to help him get control of his emotions.

"I don't know what I'll do if something happens to Darryl," he said.

"Do you know the Lord Jesus Christ?" she asked.

"Yes ma'am," he answered.

"Well I do too. I already talked to the Lord and I ain't worried about Darryl. What I'm worried about is what you might do. Vengeance is mine sayeth the Lord. Isn't that right?"

"Yes ma'am," John said.

"Will you let the Lord handle this...please?" she pleaded.

"No ma'am, I can't," he said, regaining his composure.

"Get your things together grandma, we leaving this hotel."

"You're just like that pig-headed old fool I'm married to," she fussed. "He's not saying anything, but I know he's itching to get revenge. When we arrived at the hospital and saw Darryl lying there unconscious, he just shook his head and said this won't stand woman."

After getting grandma and the girls settled into the condo John went back to the hospital. His grandpa was still there right where he left him.

"You get the women folk all taken care of?" grandpa asked.

"Yes sir," John answered. "They're having dinner at the condo right now. The girls are taking it hard but grandmas in the kitchen giving orders so they won't have too much time to worry."

"That woman sure likes to give orders," he chuckled for the first time in days.

"When am I getting out of here?" Darryl asked having just woken up.

"You got several surgeries and weeks of recovery before you can even think of going anywhere," John said. "Feel like talking?"

"Sure," Darryl replied. "I'll talk as long as they don't come and drug me."

"I know this is going to be painful, but I need to know everything you two did that day."

Darryl told as best he could remember the events leading up to the shootings. Then he remembered something.

"Mac?" he asked, and looked up at John with hope in his eyes.

"Sorry," John replied. "He was shot shortly after you left for your neighbors. Does anything stand out as unusual about that day - anything at all?" John asked.

"No, not really," Darryl said. "I do remember hearing the report from the rifle just before I blacked out. It sounded like it was a mile away."

"It was," John said.

"What else you got?" Darryl asked.

"Satellite imagery shows a car parked three miles from your house as the crow flies near the old cemetery. A check back over the past two months shows this same car parked there on 10 different occasions. Since there had been no rain, the bloodhounds were able to track him from the car to the spot where he set up to take the shot. It was exactly 1.1 miles away. This would indicate that this guy is a professional. He definitely knew what he was doing. Using ultra violet lighting, we scanned the whole area and found no signs of urine."

"What does that mean?" grandpa said.

"Means that whoever this guy was; he was a professional. He more than likely wore a Depends adult diaper. Again, this just proves that this was no dime store vigilante. There was no trace evidence at the site where he set up. Nada! Kids messing around at an old abandoned airstrip near LaGuardia found a Piper Cub with no one around. A check of the serial number revealed that this plane had been stolen from a hangar in Albany, New York – just one hour from here. Back tracking to the hangar in Albany, a car that was reported stolen two months ago from Hartford, Connecticut was found. The shots occurred at 9:15 PM. With the terrain, heavy brush and darkness, it would take the shooter 45 minutes to get to the car. That would place him back at the car at 10:00 pm. A one hour drive to Albany and then another hour's flight to the airstrip near LaGuardia would have him in the airport by midnight. We're in the process of checking all flights domestic and international that left LaGuardia after midnight that day," John said.

"What good will that do?" asked grandpa.

"Maybe nothing, but the agency has a database of known assassins. So we'll take every freeze frame photo of the passengers and cross reference them against our database as well as that of Interpol."

"What's this Interpol?" asked grandpa.

"It's the world's largest international police organization, with 188 member countries. It was created in 1923, to facilitate cross-border police co-operation, and to support and assists all organizations, authorities and services whose mission is to prevent or combat international crime. If our shooter has ever been fingerprinted and photographed, we'll get a hit. This is all assuming that he left LaGuardia and didn't drive to Baltimore, or Boston. Best bet though, is that he would want to get out of the country as quickly as possible. Grandpa, why don't you go get some rest. I need to speak with Darryl alone," John said.

After grandpa left, Jonathan stood by the bed. All this time I didn't allow myself to think of Caroline and her loss. It was too painful. Alone with Jonathan, I finally let my emotions go.

"You know I love you, the kids and grandpa and grandma," I began. "But without Caroline I don't want to live. I'm not going to ask you to help me die because I know you wouldn't. I just want to live long enough to see the bastard that hurt Caroline pay. Last night I dreamed I was holding her and telling her a story. I couldn't stop crying. The nurses came in and asked if I was in severe pain and I said yes. They increased the medication and I went out again and it's been like that since this all happened. If I'm lucid, I'm hurting so bad I can hardly breathe. John I miss her so much."

"I know bro. We'll get through this. I promise."

"Promise me one more thing," I said.

"What?" John asked.

"That you'll let me know before you do it," I said.

"I'll try, but why do you want to know before?" he asked.

"That way I'll feel a part of it," I said.

Chapter 22
Farewell My Love

Since I was still confined to the hospital and unable to travel, it was three weeks after Caroline's death that we held a quiet memorial service for Caroline in the hospital Chapel. Un-be-known to me, Caroline and the girls had picked out a beautiful urn and had made arrangements for her cremation years ago.

"Your daddy will never be able to do this," she had told the girls. "Tell him I want my ashes taken to Yellowstone."

It was a private memorial with Caroline's two aunts from Missouri – her parents were both now dead – both my cousin Michelle Horton and Jonathan's friend Dor Jerguson from North Carolina; along with Grandma, Grandpa, the girls, Jonathan and me.

With The Rose playing softly in the background, our two daughters got up, held hands, and walked to the front of the chapel where the urn with Caroline's remains sat on a table adorned with roses. They were so like their mother. Independent, strong and able do what needed to be done in the face of adversity or a tragedy.

They spoke of the good times spent with their mother and how she had prepared them for this day. They talked about Caroline's contributions and her legacy. They spoke of being witness to the most wonderful love story between their parents and I couldn't bear to even look at them.

Jonathan wheeled me up to the front and I couldn't speak a mumbling word, so great was my grief. I could only bow my head and sob.

Grandma came up and lifted my chin with her hand. "Do you believe in the Lord Jesus Christ?" she asked.
I shook my head yes and she said, "Then you're going to be alright. Bring him back to the room John."

Chapter 23

A Hit

For almost three years Jonathan had monitored Ralph Wilcox Jr's activities. He knew of Ralph's affairs with women in Helena and Bozeman. Because of constant surveillance, his war on wolves was well documented. John could have had him arrested at any time for violating the Endangered Species Act. His henchman Pedro was the main wolf killer, but Ralph had been filmed on several occasions killing wolves himself. He was an overbearing bully and poacher, but he didn't cheat on his taxes. He certainly had the means to hire a hit man, but so far he had covered his tracks well. Jonathan knew in his bones that Ralph was responsible for Caroline's death, but he had to be certain.

"We got a hit," Rebecca said when John came on the phone.

"Where are you?" John asked.

"In a cab headed to your condo. I flew into Logan 30 minutes ago," she said.

"No, don't come here," John said. "Have him drop you off at Back Bay station. It's directly across from Neiman Marcus and there's an Au Bon Pain bistro inside. I'll meet you there."

"OK," Rebecca said. She was a little disappointed as she has always wanted to meet his family.

When she walked through the doors she saw John waiving to her from a corner table. He came around the table and gave her a hug.

"Thanks for doing this Rebecca," he said.

"After three years on the job I'm still Rebecca," she said. "Well I guess it's better than agent Fleming."

"I'm sorry Becky. I'm just so wired about all this I'm not thinking straight," he said.

"I know. I'm just trying to lighten the atmosphere a little, especially in light of what I have to show you."

"Actually it was agent Hendrix from our Russian office that caught it. You remember him don't you – Vaughn Hendrix? He said you were at Annapolis together. Look here," she said as she spread some photo's out on the table. "Recognize anyone?"

John scanned the photos carefully and traced each one with his finger. He stopped on a blond gentleman with dark glasses.

"He looks familiar but I can't place him," John said.

"Think Taliban 2001. Tribal leader target #A200. Ring any bells?"

"We used him. We used him to sanction #A200. So the Taliban is behind this?" he asked.

"We don't know. All we know is that he boarded Swiss Air Flight 3210 to Zurich. From Zurich he took the rails north but we don't know where yet. We haven't been able to trace the origin, but a million dollars appeared in an account under the name of Sergei Gostov at the same time. The boys in finance say that it's almost impossible to trace and will take maybe six months to a year to unravel. The agency isn't going to pursue it at all. It's in the hands of the local sheriff and has no implications towards national security. All this information was gathered on the down low as a favor to you," she said.

"It's more than enough. How can I ever repay you for this?" John said.

"How about dinner and a movie," she said with a smile.

"You got it. As soon as this mess is ended we'll have a night on the town."

Grandma killed the idea of an open casket memorial to fake my death. Even grandpa couldn't get her to budge. She said it was blasphemy and no amount of persuasion could convince her otherwise. Now when grandpa said something and was serious, grandma would still fuss but she didn't buck. But when it came to scriptures and her Lord and Savior Jesus Christ; Mildred Perkins would not be moved. We had to just take our chances and pray there would be no more attempts on my life.

Chapter 24
Professional Courtesy

This had been a very pleasant evening. Sergei had visited his lady friend who not only prepared a delicious meal, but indulged his every sexual fantasy. As usual they ended up in the hot tub sipping a glass of vintage 2000 Cristal.

His lady friend sure knew how to live the good life. She was some sort of countess whose husband was always out of the country. Actually, Sergei's research found that he was at a chalet he kept for his mistress one village away.

Either way, it worked for him. Sometimes he found it hard to remain diligent but he was a professional. You didn't reach his status by yielding to physical urges at the risk of protocol. So it was that even if the thought appealed to him to spend the night, as was her request; protocol demanded that he leave. With a kiss goodnight and a promise to return at his earliest convenience, he departed.

As he walked up the steps leading to his door his demeanor changed. Sergei remained alive because he was always alert, wary, and totally in tune to his surroundings. He checked the pocket monitor which showed no foreign bodies inside his house. He checked the laser alarm and they were still set. The powder left under his door was undisturbed and with that final check, he put the key in the lock and turned the door knob.

As usual he entered the room in total darkness, but no matter, his sun glasses were equipped night vision goggles. He scanned the room and just as he recognized a form sitting in a chair in the corner, he heard two silencer shots fired so close together they almost sounded as one.

At the same time two nine millimeter slugs shattered both shoulders knocking him to the floor and rendering his arms useless.

Sergei had always hoped that it would end this way. His greatest fear was of being taken by some first year cop with peach fuzz on his chin. He was being taken out by someone whose skills were superior to his — and his skills were the best, or at least they used to be.

John bent down and picked up the two spent shell casings and put them in a plastic bag. He walked over to Sergei and looked down on him without speaking.

"Professional courtesy?" Sergei asked.
"If you tell me what I want to know," John answered.

After listening to Sergei's story John's nostrils were flared signifying his anger.
"Any family or friends?" John asked.
"No. You take it all," Sergei replied. "Were there children?"

"Two daughters - one's completing her Ph.D. at the University of North Carolina at Chapel Hill, and the other is a Clinical Laboratory Scientists working at a hospital in Greenville, North Carolina and hopes to go to med school. They're good kids," John said. "Like she was."

"It was business," Sergei said. "It wasn't personal."

"It's personal for you," John said. "The same person who got Caroline killed, is doing the same thing to you."

"What about unfinished business?" John continued.

"No. I take it that the one who got me in this predicament will be taken care of?" Sergei asked.

"On that, you can rest assured," John answered.

"I thought it was all over," Sergei said.

"You were good," John replied. "It took me three years."

"Take the Cheytac," Sergei said. "It's the best. There's a safe in the bedroom too. It has the numbers for all the offshore accounts. You'll have to pick the lock. I threw the key away long ago. That way I kept in practice."

In keeping his word, John ended Sergei's life with a single shot to the head - a courtesy given one professional to another.

Chapter 25
Payback

Aband of about 200 elk pawed through the fresh snow to get at the winter grass just inside the timber. In plain sight of the elk a clan of five wolves made their way down the east slope of Druid Peak into the Lamar Valley. Territorial battles and disease had reduced the Druids from a mighty clan of 27 wolves to the five that were starting the hunt today.

They were led by alpha #321, a 220 pound male and direct descendent of wolf #302 – Lamar. The pack broke into a run and started chasing the elk. This shifting and testing was designed to see if any of the elk were weak or injured. A yearling calf lagging behind the herd was quickly singled out and pulled down by the pack.

The wolves gorged themselves as the scavengers - ravens and coyotes hung around the kill. The onlookers were careful not to get too close because although down in numbers, the Druids were still unforgiving overlords who tolerated no trespassing on their kills.

A mile away the breeze brought the scent of fresh blood to the quivering nose of the boar grizzly. Before the wolves were reintroduced to Yellowstone, February would find the grizzly deep into hibernation. Now, because of the readily supply of food provided by the wolves, some grizzlies were still out and about in mid February.

The Druids had no love for grizzlies and biologist had recorded a wolf grizzly conflict that resulted in the death of a grizzly cub. A sow grizzly with two young cubs was making their way along the Lamar River. The Druids caught them in the open and surrounded the bears. The sow quickly scooped the cubs under her chin and turned to face the wolves as they charged. She would never take the bait to chase and get too far from the cubs as the Druids pressed their attack. Two wolves charged at the same time from different sides and the tactic worked. One wolf nipped her on the rump as she faced the other. She turned and chased the biter a few feet. That's all it took as both cubs were grabbed. She quickly came to the defense of one of the cubs. By this time the wolves had dragged the other cub about ten feet away. To go after that cub would mean to leave the other vulnerable. She led the remaining cub away as the Druids started to feed.

The Druids didn't give up a carcass lightly and many a young sow or yearling male grizzly were left hungry. The approaching male was six years old and no pack would prevent him from taking over a kill. He walked right up to the feeding Druids and they scattered like leaves in a wind storm.

The grizzly ate his fill in peace then retired to the timber to sleep.

Ralph Jr. stopped his horse on the ridge overlooking the valley and immediately noticed the ravens and coyotes around the carcass. He made his way down the slope with his rifle at the ready. Even if he didn't get a shot, the two bottles of strychnine in his saddlebags would do the trick. He knew that there would be ravens and coyotes that died as a result of his poisoning of the carcass, but in his mind they were just collateral damage in his never ending war on wolves. He dismounted and got ready to treat the carcass when the horse snorted and jerked the reins out of his hands and started running down the valley. He looked up just in time to see an enraged grizzly charging him full bore. He just managed to raise the rifle but was hit before he could get a shot off. Five minutes later a helicopter research team hoping to dart and re-collar some of the Druids came over the peak and saw the grizzly mauling Ralph. They buzzed the bear who left Ralph long enough to stand on his hind legs to threaten the chopper. As was always the case when working in grizzly country, the biologists were loaded for bear. Three shots from the thirty-ought-six brought the bruin down. The team quickly landed but it was too late for Ralph.

Into The Night

The local paper read: Today researchers in Yellowstone National Park witnessed the mauling of prominent Helena rancher Ralph R. Wilcox, Jr. The grizzly, a 600 pound male, was killed by the researchers but not before inflicting fatal injuries to Wilcox. Ralph R. Wilcox Jr, 58, was the only son of Bar-W founder Ralph R. Wilcox Sr.

There was no mention of the strychnine found at the scene.

Here I was back in Winston-Salem Baptist hospital for yet another surgery. It had been three years since Caroline's death and at grandma's insistence; I was having the surgery back home in North Carolina. A nice young nurse came into the room.

"You want to watch the television Mr. Glenn," she said.

"No thank you," I said.

"Can I get you anything?" she asked.

"No. I'm fine thank you," I replied.

"Well push the button if you need anything," she said as she left the room.

"I will," I said.

A few minutes later my grandpa came into the room.

"How you doing young fella?" grandpa asked.

"OK, I guess," I said.

At that time an older nurse came in to take my vitals.

"Here comes the warden," I said under my breath.

"I heard that," Miss Pat said. "Give me your arm and don't frown. Ain't nothing wrong with you anyway."

"I'm going to file a lawsuit," I said.

"File one," Miss Pat said. "See if I care. And turn that TV on. I want to see the parade. You know the Panthers won the Super Bowl and Charlotte's going crazy."

"So how's my grandson doing?" grandpa asked.

"Your grandson is spoiled and he's got half the nurses here scared. But now if that new nurse from Pittsburgh with the pretty smile and dimples comes in – oh he's a different camper then."

I was so mad I could eat nails when she said that. Marva was a nice person, but I was still in love with Caroline and there was no room for any other thoughts in my mind. I had heard nothing from Jonathan in six months and was really feeling cranky. What I didn't need was some matchmaking nurse to start unfounded rumors. Grandpa saw the anger rising in me as said to Miss Pat, "Good. Someone needs to make him smile," and he winked at me.

The tickertape parade for the Super Bowl champion Carolina Panthers was just finishing up at city hall in downtown Charlotte. The team was on the grand stand now and it looked as if the whole state was out in force supporting the Panthers. One player after another stepped up to the podium to address the crowd. Next up was the pride of Winston Salem State University and Super Bowl XXV MVP Julius Price. Caroline had despised him until the day she died, but I always thought it was neat that a WSSU alum was making it big in the NFL. And now, thanks to the exploits of J.P. in helping the Panthers to win their first Super Bowl; my beloved alma mate would be back on top and I could talk junk to those Ram haters –the A&T Aggies just down interstate 40.

J.P. stepped up to the mike and the crowd went wild. The Panthers had defeated the New England Patriots 28 to 21 in what was one of the most watched Super Bowls in history. J.P. had returned a punt for a touchdown in the first quarter and another in the fourth. With two minutes remaining and the score tied at 21, the Patriots had the ball first and ten on the Panthers 40 yard line. It appeared that Moss had J.P. beat on a slant pattern but with that remarkable speed he was known for; J.P. made up the ground and intercepted the ball on the five yard line. What happened next can only be described as "Prime Time-esq." Like Deion in his prime, J.P. weaved his way ninety-five yards for the game winning touchdown. He had all the trappings of a YBM (Young Black Millionaire) – the diamond earrings, the bling-bling around his neck and on his fingers, and hordes of adoring fans. He still had somewhat of a nasty attitude and fancied himself as some sort of gangster rapper, but today he was king and the world his playground.

"WHAT'S UP CHARLOTTEEEEEE?" he shouted and thrust the mike into the air as the chorus of JP! JP! JP! - could be heard coming from the crowd. He went on to thank the Lord for giving him the talent, his parents for bringing him into this world to make it a better place, and his former coaches for believing in him. Then he put him index finger to his lips and motioned for the crown to be quiet.

My cell phone rang and it was John.
"Well it's about time," I said.
"I know," he said. "I've been real busy. Are you watching the parade?"
"Yeah," I said. "Hold on a minute. J.P.'s going to speak."

"Bring them TV cameras in close," J.P. said. "I got some words for the haters."

The cameras zoomed in close and you could see the platinum in his teeth.

"Hand me that freaking trophy," he demanded. "Like I said, I got some words for you haters. LOOK AT ME NOW HATERS!"

He raised both hands above his head and the crowd went wild. Then, with a snarl on his face, he leaned in close to the microphone and said, "This message is for my number one fan. Paybacks a bitch! Ain't it Hillbilly?"

He then pointed his finger at the camera and made the motion as if pulling the trigger on a gun. Next, he held that same mangled finger up to his lips, and blew on it as if he were blowing smoke from a gun barrel.

I couldn't believe what I had just heard. The monitor was going off the chart as my blood pressure skyrocketed.

"It was him? It was J.P.? All this time I thought it was Ralph Wilcox and it was Julius Price?" I screamed into the cell.
"Shhhh," Jonathan whispered, "You'll spoil the moment."

The cameras were still zoomed in on J.P.'s face and the ABC feed was showing him in slow motion. As I watched closely a red dot appeared in the center of his forehead. It reminded me of a laser pointer dot, like the ones used in a power point presentation. Seconds later, a hole replaced the laser dot and J.P. started to fall backwards.

He was dead before he hit the stage. Pandemonium broke out as everyone dove for cover. No one heard the report from the rifle - it was too far away. I looked at the screen in silence as my tears started their cheek slide. It seemed as if time stood still until I heard Jonathan's voice.

"You OK?" Jonathan said.

"Do you know that I love you?" I said.

"Do you know I love you more?" he replied.

Epilogue

A substantial gift in excess of 2 million dollars was given to Winston Salem State University in the name of Dr. Caroline A. Glenn. The donor, an un-named benefactor from Switzerland, wished to remain anonymous. Subsequently, the building that housed the zoology department, was renamed the Caroline A Glenn building and a portrait of Dr. Glenn and her beloved wolf, Lamar, adorned the entrance wall.

A dual memorial service was held on campus to honor and remember WSSU's two most famous alums: World renowned wolf biologist Dr. Caroline A Glenn, and Super Bowl XXV MVP Julius Price. Both tragically cut down by a sniper's bullet at the height of their careers.

Dr Glenn's husband, who himself is a WSSU alum - Dr. Darryl A. Glenn, did not to attend the service. No other members of the Glenn family were in attendance.

Darryl rode in silence up the east side of Druid Peak. He stopped when he got to the bluff overlooking the Lamar

Valley and dismounted. The wind was barely stirring as he reached into his saddlebags and took our Caroline's urn and a small cassette player. Next, he walked to the edge of the bluff and placed the cassette player on bare rock. This was a spot where he and Caroline had often sat while glassing the valley below for wolves. One tear forced another from the ledge of his eyes as he pushed the play button on the cassette. He stood there in silence with the Rose playing softly in the background. The tears continued their migration down his cheek as he opened the lid and poured his beloved Caroline into the breeze. As if on cue, the wind picked up and Caroline's ashes were carried out over the Lamar Valley. Darryl placed the urn on the ground next to the cassette player, mounted, and started riding back down the trail.

Later that night, under the light of a full moon, wolf #321 – alpha leader of the Druid Peak pack, sniffed the urn then lifted his head and howled into the night.

LaVergne, TN USA
18 August 2010
193805LV00001B/37/P